LUCID DREAMER

M.R. KENNOR

Dedicated to R.G. Kennor, aka Dad.

"Only in our dreams are we free. The rest of the time we need wages."

TERRY PRATCHETT, WRYD SISTERS

CHAPTER 1

A blurry image appeared. It was dark and gloomy. Shadowy with textures and outlines overlapped. Cars roaring past, pedestrians flowing by, noises heard from everywhere. There was a surreal echoing clamour of engines... people talking... wind howling...pigeons landing and flying away, although none of it was clear by itself. The noises collectively made an incoherent, almost thundering roar that continued relentlessly. It was a busy town centre. A figure could be seen moving past. It somehow stood out from the rest of the hustling crowd of faceless pedestrians, but why? What made this person stand out in the crowd? It quickly became apparent.

The figure was moving at a noticeably quicker speed than everyone else. It was a person running and clearly anxious to be somewhere else some time ago while the rest of the crowd were moving at a considerably slower pace, not quite so concerned with moving at speed. The figure was weaving in and out of other people to avoid collision, stepping out onto the road at times as the only way to avoid the crowds when there was nowhere else on the pavement to overtake or evade the oncoming pavement users. The figure quickly approached a side street along the pavement, people surrounding on all sides. The figure remained focussed on advancing forward, never peering to the side – vision obscured by the sheer volume of footfalls. The figure rushed out from the crowd on to the road to cross over. At the same time a speeding car flew out of nowhere and turned the corner where the figure was crossing. Tyres screeched as a loud thud was heard and passers-by looked on. There was an almighty eruption in the crowds. Some gasped, others screamed in horror, while some swore and cursed in shock, all at the same time. The figure lay motionless in the middle of the road.

Another blurry image appeared, this time no clearer than the last, but certainly more civilised. Pleasant music could be heard... it was of an orchestra. A figure could be heard making a peculiar babel, coughing perhaps. There were people... people settled on chairs around a table...several tables... many tables. A figure could be made out coughing again. What looked like men in suits and tuxedos... women in dresses...figures were walking around the tables carrying objects...trays...trays of food...drinks...bottles and glasses. Were they waiters in a restaurant? The coughing noise was detected again. The civilised ambiance in the restaurant quickly turned sour as all attention was locked on to the figure coughing. The figure was not coughing, they were choking. It was a man, choking on some food lodged in his throat. Panicking, the man rose from his chair. All the other figures gazed on in shock and horror. Another figure, a woman someone sitting next to the man screamed for someone to help. The figure gasped for breath. One of the waiters nearby tried to slap the figure on the back, hoping that would solve the problem. The figure continued to gasp for air. The waiter tried slapping the figure on the back again, yet nothing happened. The waiter tried again, and again, and again, still with no success. By this time the figure was becoming increasingly desperate for air and the other figures in the restaurant, particularly those on the same table, appeared to become increasingly hysterical. A figure from another table darted forward and tried repeating the waiter's idea of slapping the victim on the back, only this time harder, still with no success. The victim tumbled to the floor and collapsed.

A third blurry image appeared. It was high up, there were figures in very distinctive clothing. Distinctive looking hats....hard hats. Jackets of a distinctive colour...a bright colour...a florescent colour. There were wooden planks...steel...steel structures...scaffolding. Figures were moving around carrying things...tools... working... very busy. Some kind of construction work. A figure was seen climbing high, very high, higher than anyone else, yet no-one was paying attention. Everyone else was too swamped in performing their own tasks. Some were in groups, others by themselves. The figure continued to ascend higher and higher. The figure reached the top, for some reason they slipped, and fell. At this point everyone turned to look. Pandemonium ensued. Figures were running everywhere screaming and shouting. Within seconds the incident was bought to everyone's attention.

A young lady was fast asleep in her bed. Sleeping heavily it was far from peaceful. All of a sudden she awoke, letting out a mighty scream, sitting up she was in a heavy sweat. She was having nightmares. These were all her nightmares. She contemplated her predicament in which she realised that she was now safe in bed and that the whole ordeal had just been a bad dream. She glanced over at her glow-in-the-dark alarm clock to see the time. It read 03:34. She remembered her job interview that she had to attend at 9.30 that morning and that she would need to get up no later than 08.00 to get ready and arrive there on time. She had previously set the alarm for 07.50 to allow her to snooze for ten minutes. After realising she had plenty of time, she relaxed and lay back down again.

Her endeavour to fall back to sleep proved futile. Her mind could not stop thinking about the subject of her dreams that she recalled so vividly. Were they really dreams? She thought to herself. They seemed so real. She lay in her bed pondering on why she was having these dreams and what they could mean, if anything. She had never experienced anything quite like this until recently.

Despite her efforts to ignore these thoughts she couldn't shake off her worries. She was unable to ignore her anxieties and the emotion she felt was too great for her to fall asleep. She lay in her bed unable to nod off for some considerable time. She gazed over again at her alarm clock, it read 05.47. Over two hours had passed and it was now becoming a worry also that she would miss out on too much sleep, or worse still that she would oversleep and miss arriving at her interview on time. This ironically made falling asleep harder still.

CHAPTER 2

RING-RING!! RING-RING!! RING-RING!! The young lady's alarm clock chimed off. To her it bellowed like a burglar alarm in her ears. How can it go off now? She thought to herself. It's far too early. It must have been set for the wrong time. She reached out her hand, grabbed the alarm clock and launched it across the room. The clock smashed against the wall on the opposite side. The alarm stopped and she instantly nodded off again.

Knock! Knock! A noise from the door echoed through her room. The door slowly opened and another young lady revealed herself from around the other side.

'Hello!!' the young lady said, with a certain air of stupidity. 'Haven't you got to get up?' she asked.

The young lady in bed slowly turned her head up, without moving her body glanced over to where the alarm clock was, then suddenly remembered. She threw it across the room just a moment ago. Or was it only a moment ago?

Still not fully awake and only partially opening

her eyes her attention now turned to the lady at the door.

'What time is it?' she uttered barely comprehensively and in a slurry voice.

'Brooke it's 8.30, you have to be at your job interview in an hour!!' replied the young lady. At that point Brooke shot up out of bed in a panic.

'Shit!!' she screamed. 'I didn't realise it was this late!'

The young lady at the door began to laugh. Brooke started clambering around the bedroom grabbing at her stuff then realised she needed to take a bath.

The tidiness of her bedroom otherwise was as immaculate as it was pristine. No expense was spared obtaining the finest quality furniture. The room was coloured mostly in black and white, with multi-colour trimmings.

'Forget it' she said, 'I haven't even got time for a quick shower'. 'Ricki' she said, addressing the young lady at the door. 'Make me some coffee will you?'

Slowly turning around and heading out towards the kitchen to do as Brooke asked she continued to chuckle away. This was all a big joke to her, laughing at other people's little hiccups. Brooke was actually the same and if the roles were reversed she would laugh at her equally in this situation too.

In the bedroom Brooke was still scurrying around looking for everything. She put on her smart suit and shoes then dashed into the bathroom. She decided to take a 'student shower'. She sprayed herself liberally with deodorant then tied her long brown hair back in a ponytail, quick and easy. She didn't bother putting on her make-up. She never wore it much anyway. She had no need for it. Her fresh faced appearance made her look even younger than her twenty five years.

Brooke then rushed to the kitchen where Ricki had finished making her coffee. The decor of the kitchen, much like the rest of the apartment was pristine. A softly coloured décor made the room illuminate dazzlingly. Were it not for the pile of dishes and the eyesore of clutter left behind it could easily be mistaken for a show home display.

Brooke grabbed a cereal bar from the cupboard and began chewing it, not gradual and noiselessly but rapidly with large mouthfuls. Ricki handed her the cup of coffee which she started drinking while still munching on her cereal bar. 'Thanks', she then blurted out with her mouth full of both coffee and mushy cereal bar. Standing five foot and six inches tall, she remained on her feet throughout.

Ricki, still with a beaming smirk on her face, then started enquiring

'What's with all this then, I mean me getting you

up in the morning? You're supposed to be the responsible older sister, it's usually you doing this sort of thing for me!'

To which Brooke replied, after swallowing her food, 'I had trouble sleeping'.

Ricki's facial expression then morphed to a more serious look. 'You been getting those dreams again?' she asked.

'Yeah' said Brooke. 'I remember them so well too, I saw...I saw people...people dying again. It was horrible.'

'I think they could be scenes from a film you watched,' said Ricki.

'I don't know' said Brooke while waving her hand dismissively. 'I can't worry about that now, I need to focus on this interview.' She continued, 'I....we need this job. Our savings won't last forever and I wanna make sure we have a steady stream of cash coming into this household long before that money runs out.'

Brooke had been searching for a job for several months now and this was the first interview she'd had in weeks. An extremely clever young lady, she had always been top of her class at school in every academic subject. Brooke had enjoyed a well-paid job as a market analyst but due to unfortunate circumstances beyond her control she was made redundant several months ago.

She then looked at the clock on the wall. It read 08:35. She guzzled down the rest of her coffee, 'I've really got to go now,' she said.

Brooke put her cup down, grabbed her bag and phone then proceeded to walk out.

'Good luck' Ricki shouted out as Brooke slammed the front door behind her. 'What would mum and dad say?' Ricki uttered to herself as she sat down at the table, her coffee cup in hand.

CHAPTER 3

Ricki was sitting on the sofa still in her pyjamas with her feet up watching TV. This was very typical of her. She was rather lazy and somewhat of a slob. An empty coffee cup and bowl stood on the table next to her. She too was unemployed, a little bit unmotivated and clearly less keen on finding a new job than her sister. It was as if she was waiting for something to happen that she really enjoyed, and that she could do well. Every job she had done so far was either too boring or too stressful for her.

Twenty one years old Ricki was blonde and of similar height and slim build to Brooke, though not identical she sported many similar features that made it evident they were sisters. The two of them also shared many, but not all interests. They were the same yet somewhat different.

Brooke stormed back in through the front door, slammed it shut and let out an enormous sigh.

'How did it go'? Ricki shouted out.

Brooke made her way in to the living room remaining silent, threw her bag down and fell in to the armchair near to Ricki. She breathed out heavily.

'Well?' asked Ricki'.

'It was a disaster' said Brooke.

'What happened?' asked Ricki insistently.

'Well to start with', she said, 'I was late by about five minutes, which despite me trying to blame it on abnormally heavy traffic was a stigma that stayed with me throughout the whole interview.'

'Well how did it go otherwise'? asked Ricki.

'OK I think', replied Brooke, 'I answered all the questions pretty well but I could tell the woman who interviewed me was put-off right from the start.' She added.

'Well it could have been worse', said Ricki, 'At least you made it to the interview. If your clever little sister hadn't woken you from your eternal slumber you wouldn't have made it at all!'

'Yeah, thanks' said Brooke.

'You did your best and that's all you can do', said Ricki. 'I mean what's the worst that can happen? You don't get the job? If not I'm sure you'll find another one soon enough,' she continued.

'I guess you're right', said Brooke.

Now more relaxed she started to forget about the job interview and glanced around at the room, at Ricki, then at her empty cup and bowl on the table.

'I see you've had a hard day!' she said to Ricki quite sarcastically. 'Have you even moved off that sofa this morning?' she asked.

'Yes I went to the bathroom once or twice!' answered Ricki.

Ricki's laziness and general lack of responsibility was something that always bothered Brooke since they were children. She was always the one who in some way or other had to look after her younger sister and try and keep her out of trouble. She always felt that she had to clear up after her, both figuratively and literally. She owned the apartment they lived in and allowed her little sister to stay with her indefinitely. Since Brooke knew that Ricki had nowhere else to go there was no way she would leave her own flesh and blood out on the street, besides which her sister was also her best friend and she was thrilled to have the company.

Brooke had always regarded purchasing a home of her own as a top priority and knew that with soaring property values the place was also a very good investment, even when considering the ludicrous price she had to pay for it. The accommodation was a three bedroom apartment that was part of a listed building in one of the most sought after streets in Kensington, London. She had acquired the mortgage for the property outright herself and put almost all her wages from her previous employment into paying for it.

'We've got stuff to do today' insisted Brooke, 'We need to tidy up this place, put the rubbish out and get some shopping'.

Brooke stood up, marched to the kitchen and started to clear away the dirty dishes lying around. Ricki slowly rose to her feet, picked up her empty cup and bowl then strolled casually into the kitchen after her. Brooke picked up some rubbish and made her way to the bin to dump it. Ricki saw her approach the bin and panicked. She did her damnedest to cut in front of Brooke and take the rubbish from her hand before she opened the bin.

'I'll put that in the bin' she said - Too late!

Brooke opened the bin before Ricki had a chance to cut in front of her. She peered inside and was clearly disgruntled at what she saw before her.

Brooke picked up a handful of cans, plastic bottles and newspapers that were lying visibly on top of all the other rubbish.

'What the hell is this!!?' she demanded.

Ricki laughed nervously with a cheeky grin on her face.

'Who left that there!?' she said, trying nervously to make a joke of it.

'This is all the recycling you were supposed to put out yesterday' exclaimed Brooke 'You were supposed to sort through it and put it out separately into different bins outside', she continued.

Brooke then continued rummaging through the bin picking out more and more items that Ricki was meant to recycle.

'Look at all this stuff!' she said while picking more items up one at a time. 'Why don't you bother recycling these? Is it really that much trouble to spend a few minutes sorting through it!?'

'Oh come on' said Ricki, 'Stop fussing, it's just a few empty cans and bottles, it's not like the world's gonna end because I put a few cans in with the rubbish!'.

'That's totally the wrong attitude!' Brooke argued. 'If everyone had that attitude then no-one would ever recycle'. She continued.

'OK, OK, I'll put the recycling away in future' replied Ricki, now caving in knowing that she was fighting a losing battle with her sister.

The two young ladies finished clearing up then made sandwiches for lunch and sat down on the sofa to watch TV while they ate. While tucking into her sandwich Ricki continued to enquire more about Brooke's dreams.

'So tell me more about what you see in these dreams then', she asked.

The TV began broadcasting the lunchtime news in the background with the intro music, but neither Brooke nor Ricki were paying much attention. Brooke then began.

'I remember three very different scenarios that I had last night. They're dark and misty but still quite clear. The first one was a figure running fast along a busy street, like they're in a big rush. A man I think....I see them running through the busy street avoiding the other people on the path. The figure then runs out in front of a moving car and gets hit.'

Immediately after Brooke explained the incident the newsreader on the TV made an announcement introducing a tragic accident;

'There has been severe delays for commuters travelling to Hounslow due to road closures following a fatal incident in which a man was killed today after being hit by a car along Hounslow Central in west London. The person has not yet been identified but it is believed he is a local resident. A part of the streets surrounding the incident have also been closed off.......

The ladies gaped at each other in awe.

'Shit! That's so freaky!' said Ricki. Brooke then sat there appearing very apprehensive and disturbed. 'What are the chances of that happening eh!?' She added.

Brooke remained silent. Ricki, now aware of her

sister's mood was thinking of something re-assuring to say. She thought it was just a bizarre co-incidence and wasn't going to start believing her dreams were really some kind of prophecy.

'Don't worry, I'm sure it's just co-incidence' she said. Despite her sister's sincerest efforts Brooke continued to feel increasingly adjitated.

CHAPTER 4

The ladies both finished their lunches, albeit slower than usual. Brooke, though clearly distressed, did not let the situation de-rail her plans for the day.

'Let's go shopping'. She uttered out of the blue.

'Yes I could do with some new clothes!' joked Ricki.

'I meant food shopping!' insisted Brooke.

'OK Shall I book a taxi?' asked Ricki.

'No!' Brooke replied sternly. She continued insistently, 'We have this argument every time we leave the house!' 'We can take the bus, it's cheaper and it's quiet at this time, and if we leave soon we can get there and back in time before those horrible school kids come out!'

Ricki rolled her eyes in disapproval. They both collected their stuff together ready to go out.

They left the house and walked to the local bus stop. The bus arrived almost immediately. It was empty save an elderly couple seated at the front. Ricki boarded first and deliberately headed straight to the back to sit down as far away as possible from the other people, with Brooke following closely behind her. The journey was a good 10-15 minutes at the best of times so Ricki knew she had time to finally talk to her sister properly.

'So', Ricki began. 'Tell me what else happened in the other dreams'.

'Well', said Brooke. 'There's this other dream where I'm in a restaurant, or at least I think I'm there, I don't really remember walking or moving around normally, it's like I'm almost sort of...floating. I'm like a ghost with all this stuff happening around me. It feels so real. I see a restaurant full of people and someone...a man possibly, starts choking. There's these people all around him, they try and help him but can't. They're all trying to slap him on the back, there's people panicking and screaming around him and I think he dies.'

'Shit!' says Ricki. 'That sounds messed up. What else did you dream of?'

Brooke took a few seconds to reflect. She then began to describe the third dream.

'I was on a building site' she said. 'There were men in hard hats everywhere, there's scaffolding and men working up high. There's this one guy who climbs up really high, like higher than anyone else to the top of the scaffolding, then he loses his balance and falls'. Ricki began to ponder for a minute.

'So.... are you floating around there as well?' She then asked.

'I think so' replied Brooke. 'It's a strange feeling, it's like I'm there but I'm not there' she continued. 'None of the other people can see me.'

The bus arrived at the stop near the supermarket where the ladies both got off. It was next to a small row of shops and businesses along the street they had to walk past in order to reach the store.

They continued for a short distance along the road where they noticed something was happening.

Right away the two sisters could see something was wrong. There was an ambulance parked nearby and a large crowd of people had accumulated near the shops. They looked around at all the people and could hear whispers and murmurings. The ladies tried to weave in and out of everyone blocking their way to the supermarket and as they got deeper into the crowd it quickly became denser and denser with people. They approached the entrance outside the Italian restaurant.

All of a sudden two ambulance paramedics walked out in front of them wheeling what looked like a body covered under a blanket. The body was motionless. The sudden, almost eerie silence and the look on everyone's faces, including those of the paramedics said everything. The paramedics went round the back of the ambulance, pushed the wheelie bed on then climbed aboard. They shut the doors behind them and the ambulance drove away.

Brooke turned to a lady nearby.

'What happened here?' she asked the lady.

'Apparently some guy choked to death' she said. 'He was eating with his friends in the restaurant, then he started choking then everyone came to his aid but no-one could help. First the waiter tried to slap him on the back then some other guy but there was nothing they could do, poor guy fell to the ground, he was only a young man too.'

Brooke and Ricki both turned white. They looked at each other with a mixture of shock, horror and disbelief, in equal measure. Each of them knew exactly what the other one was thinking.

They walked away from the crowd. Brooke turned to Ricki.

'Right, tell me it's just a co-incidence now!' she insisted.

Ricki was still in denial about the whole thing.

'OK, I'll admit this is really freaky' she said. 'But I still think it's just one of those freaky incidents, I mean what are you trying to say? That you predicted this, that you saw this very incident happen in your dreams a few hours ago!!?'

'Yes that's exactly what I'm thinking' said Brooke.

'What are the chances of anyone seeing this before it happens?' she continued.

'Right, I'll admit it's bizarre but I'm sure there's a rational explanation for it all' replied Ricki.

'How can you be so dismissive!?' asked Brooke 'We have seen two incidents happen within hours of each other and I'm telling you I saw them both happen in my dream!!' she insisted.

Ricki stared back at Brooke and thought for a moment. 'OK...right...look' she said. 'Let's just assume for now they were both just amazing co-incidences. These things are freaky but they happen'.

Brooke rested down on a nearby bench to gather her thoughts.

'It's real, I know it is'. She said, staring down at the ground.

Ricki sat down next to her. Looking at Brooke she took a deep breath.

'OK, how about we say that if we see any more of your visions come true again we'll take that as full and final? She suggested. 'Once is a co-incidence, twice is suspicious, three times is a certainty' she continued. 'We can even research it when we get home' she added. 'We'll watch every news channel and check every website to make sure'.

Brooke paused, reflecting on her response. 'OK' she said. 'But if we find out for sure I'm gonna need you to support me in this' she added.

Ricki turned and looked Brooke in the eyes. 'OK I'll be with you all the way' she said. 'What will you do if you find out these dreams are really real?' she asked her.

'I don't know' replied Brooke.

CHAPTER 5

The ladies arrived back home with all their shopping. A newspaper had been delivered and was lying inside the hallway on the floor. Brooke, rather uncharacteristically, dumped her shopping bags in the kitchen immediately while Ricki was forced involuntarily, to put all the shopping away. Picking up the newspaper she then proceeded to read the front cover while it was resting on the small hallway table. The main story in bold lettering was an article about the Euro lottery jackpot reaching an all-time high of £200 million. Despite this story seeming irrelevant she felt compelled to read it. 'How I'd love to win all that money!' she said to herself.

An extremely fast reader, Brooke could scrutinise the whole article just by scrawling her finger quickly down the page and cast an eye over every word that was written. She stood in the hallway leaning over the small table to wade through the article, then the whole newspaper, yet she found nothing that related to her search.

Brooke then entered the living room to switch on

the TV. She turned on her laptop and sat down on the sofa in front of the TV with the computer on her lap. She began flicking through every channel on the TV looking for news while her laptop was booting up. Brooke ploughed through all the mainstream channels but none of them were showing news at the time. News was not broadcast much at that time of day. It was too late for lunchtime and too early for the evening. She then turned the TV over to BBC News 24.

Brooke's laptop booted up and she began to peruse every news website she could think of on the internet. BBC, ITV, Channel 4, Channel 5, Sky News, Yahoo News, Google News, Mail Online, the Guardian and more. Ricki made her way in shortly after and sat down with her tablet to assist Brooke. They scoured through each and every website for any resemblance of a story that matched her third dream. They used Google Search, Bling Search, Blekko, Boardreader, Quantcast, Duckduck Go and more. They checked local, regional and even national news sites for any story that it might resemble. They searched and searched and searched, and searched for hours, all while listening to the TV, but found no recent news story that matched Brooke's dream.

With each website she visited Brooke slowly became less convinced that her dreams were real. After several hours of hard searching they both decided that they had looked enough. They put their computers aside and continued to watch TV until the 6 o' clock news came on, still nothing. They then watched the regional news, again still nothing.

Ricki stood up from off the sofa next to Brooke.

'Let's have some dinner' she said.

'Yeah, OK' replied Brooke.

'Shall we order some take away?' asked Ricki.

Taking a very dim view of what Ricki had just said Brooke gazed at Ricki as if to show her complete disapproval. 'We don't need to order anything, we've just bought a fridge full of food!' she exclaimed.

'Get something out the fridge or freezer for us. Pizza will do for me' she added.

Ricki took the cooking duties upon herself and prepared pizza for them both. Seated in the kitchen the ladies ate their dinner at the table with the distant noise of the TV still resounding in the background.

'Maybe you're right' said Brooke. 'Maybe those dreams were just dreams, and nothing more' she continued. 'It's just that...you know I could have sworn they were real. The dreams I had last night were the most vivid I've ever had' she said.

'You didn't eat a lot of cheese did you?' asked Ricki. 'They say cheese can give you weird dreams if you eat it before you go to bed'.

'No' Brooke said smiling. 'I don't recall eating cheese or any other diary based products before bedtime!' she added.

Both ladies began to relax and enjoy their pizza. They were after all very hungry after their long tiring day, particularly Brooke. She remembered she'd also had her job interview that day, which now seemed like a distant memory. Ricki also recalled the other events of that day, including Brooke's interview.

'So when do you hear about your interview', she asked.

'Dunno' said Brooke. 'They told me they have a few more people to see over the next couple of days so I should hear from them within the next week or so', she continued.

'That's quite a long time to wait isn't it', said Ricki 'I've never had to wait more than a day or so after my job interviews' she added.

Brooke just shrugged. 'If I'm not successful then I'll just keep on looking' she said. 'You should do the same' she added quite insistently.

The distant sound of the TV in the living room grew louder as the music for the evening news sounded through the flat into the kitchen. Continuing their conversation without paying too much attention the news carried on throughout their discussion.

'Yes I will, I'll get back on the internet first thing tomorrow and start looking at jobs again' said Ricki. 'I'll go through that newspaper again as well' she added.

'Good' replied Burke.

At that moment the newsreader on TV made an announcement;

'News just in...A construction site in East London was closed off today following an accident in which a building worker was killed after falling ten floors to the ground. Exact details of the accident are yet to be confirmed but it is believed that the builder tripped and fell to his death after climbing a ladder...'

The ladies, upon hearing the report, gaped at each other in horror as they had done twice already that day. They shot up and dashed into the living room to watch the TV. Ricki grabbed the remote to turn up the sound while they stood there listening, the news caster continued;

'The man was said to be one of the youngest members of his workforce and one of their newest team members. It is believed that he had made a dangerous mistake while working at the construction yard without the proper equipment. The construction company have yet to officially confirm the man's identity and we shall provide more details of the incident as it comes in. In other news this weekend's Euro lottery

main draw is thought to top £200 million, the largest ever in UK lottery history.....'

Tumbling back on to the sofa Brooke looked unreservedly scared and demoralised, her face now white with terror. Ricki stood still for a moment then sat down next to her. She grabbed her hand as a way of comforting and trying to re-assure both Brooke, and herself. Ricki was now as mortified as her sister.

'What shall we do?' asked Ricki. There was silence for a few seconds.

'I don't know' Brooke replied. 'I really, really don't know'.

CHAPTER 6

That night Brooke stayed up well into the early hours of the morning, afraid of falling asleep. She had fallen into a frantic and isolated state of mind, lonely and afraid. This incident had changed her. She could no longer face falling asleep due to fear of having any more vivid dreams. She drank lots of coffee with sugar as a way of keeping tiredness away. Whenever she started feeling in any way sleepy she would get up and walk around in order to keep herself active. Ricki sat with her, she could have gone to bed at any time but felt the need to stay by her sister's side to try and offer her some comfort and support.

'You can't just fight tiredness off like some kind of enemy' Ricki said. 'Sooner or later you're gonna have to go to sleep'. She continued.

'I can't' replied Brooke. 'I'm too scared!' she added. 'I can't face any more of those dreams knowing that they are real'.

Ricki couldn't argue with that. She completely understood her sister's fear and knew that she herself would feel exactly the same.

Several hours passed by with Brooke becoming increasingly tired and exhausted. The night had come and gone. Daylight was again visible outside. Ricki, despite some attempt to stay awake, had now been asleep for several hours and this had made Brooke feel even more alone and terrified. She continued to drink coffee and stay active, at this point staying on her feet she tried walking around. She wandered into the kitchen to the tap several times to throw cold water on her face in a vain attempt to stay refreshed. She tried slapping herself around the face and knocking on her head with her fist thinking that the pain would help keep her awake.

In the end it inevitably proved futile. She reached the point where she could no longer stand the exhaustion. The tiredness had now become physically painful. Brooke had never deprived herself of sleep like this before. Eventually deciding to sit down and rest she was so tired that the sofa had never been so comfortable to her. She reluctantly fell back effortlessly sinking her head and neck into the soft cushions of the sofa. She was terrified emotionally but had to admit that the physical comfort she felt at this point was a wonderful sensation. Her eyes closed within moments and she lay there still. All efforts to stay awake had now come to an end as she almost instantly fell fast asleep.

CHAPTER 7

Brooke woke up in a heavy sweat and let out a mighty scream, much like the one from the day before. At that point Ricki, sitting next to her on the sofa also jumped out of her skin with the sudden jolt of noise. Both ladies looked at each other and quickly realised the state of the situation.

'Christ! You scared the crap out of me!' said Ricki.

'Sorry' replied Brooke. 'I had more dreams again' she added.

'What happened this time?' asked Ricki.

'Don't ask!' Brooke replied sternly.

The next few days Brooke spent most nights repeating what she had done the night before. Drinking coffee, eating large quantities of sugar and making every effort to stay awake for as long as possible. It was all in vain. She could only keep the tiredness at bay for so long. She would only sleep for one to two hours per night but it was just long enough for her to dream her visions then wake up again. Her health and wellbeing, not to mention her personal hygiene began to suffer. She had changed. She was no longer the outgoing, confident and happy young lady she was before. She was broken, depressed, anxious, weary, and above all else terrified.

Ricki was forced to suffer watching her big sister deteriorate first hand and after several days felt that she really had to do something. She walked in to the living room to join Brooke as they watched a film on TV. It was the very final moments of the film Spiderman.

'What if your dreams are a gift to you?' she says. 'What if it's something you could use to your advantage, or for the help of others? All these people you see, they're people that need help. What if you could help them, what if you could be there when they need you?'

Brooke sat there and shook her head continuously.

'No' she said.

'You could do so much good with this gift if you learnt to use it properly' insisted Ricki.

Brooke shot up from the sofa. 'NO!' she yelled, before proceeding towards the door.

Ricki saw where she was headed, leapt up then darted round the opposite way to block her sister before she exited the room. She stood in front of Brooke and carried on at her.

'You can't keep living like this, you have to face up to your problem and do something about it!' said

Ricki.

Brooke pushed Ricki to one side then brushed against her as she side stepped past her and stormed out towards her room. Now rather annoyed at her big sister, both for pushing past her and for her ignorance and cowardice in facing her dilemma Ricki dashed out behind Brooke and continued to rant at her.

'You can't carry on living like this. There are people out there suffering and dying and you're sitting around this flat doing nothing to help them!!'

Brooke ignored her and carried on with her march towards the bedroom. She entered her room and slammed the door behind her without saying another word. Ricki walked up to the door and shouted through it to her

'You know I'm right' she exclaimed. 'You can't continue this forever. I want to help you. Let me help you in any way I can'.

Brooke remained silent.

'What would mum and dad say!?' added Ricki.

'PISS OFF!!' shouted Brooke through the door.

Ricki was by now very upset at the way her big sister was acting. She turned around and headed back to the living room where she began to cry.

Brooke locked her bedroom door shut behind her

then fell on to her bed looking at the ceiling. She then realised her predicament that she could easily fall asleep in this position and instantly jumped up again. She gazed around the room to her chair then walked over and sat down. Her emotions now got the better of her. She began to sob, loudly.

CHAPTER 8

An hour passed since the two sisters argued. After slowly rising up out of her chair Brooke quietly opened her bedroom door then made her way to the living room where she could hear Ricki watching TV. She walked to the entrance of the door and glanced over at Ricki in front of the TV. Ricki heard Brooke approaching and turned around to see her sister standing at the doorway, eyes red raw with tears and snot running down from her nose.

'I'm sorry!' admitted Brooke holding out her arms towards her younger sister. Ricki also teary eyed stood up and staggered around towards her.

'I'm sorry too' she said. Standing face to face inside the doorway the sisters hugged each other. 'I'm so sorry, I've been a complete bitch to you' added Brooke.

'It's OK' replied Ricki. 'Just don't shut me out any longer, let me help you' she added.

'I will' replied Brooke convincingly.

After a long and tearful hug together the two sisters rested down on the sofa next to each other.

'You were right' said Brooke 'I can't keep cowering away from all my dreams. If I can somehow help these people I see in my dreams then I should do it. I just have to figure out how'.

Ricki smiled at Brooke who then looked back at her somewhat intrigued.

'I have an idea' said Ricki. 'Have you ever heard of the ability of lucid dreaming?' she asked.

'Err...no' replied Brooke 'What's that?'

'It's the power to have control of your dreams. In your dreams that you've had you say you can see things like you're actually there, so what if you could truly see everything you needed to so you could know exactly when and where all these events happen?' said Ricki. 'If you can figure out where all these horrible things are happening then maybe you can get there before they happen and stop them' added Ricki.

Brooke looked puzzled. 'OK, firstly how do I go about taking control of my dreams, and secondly how do I figure out when and where each one is?'

Ricki paused for a moment.

'Well I've got an idea about how you could learn to control your dreams. I just don't know about how you find the time and place, but you're supposed to be the smart one, you'll figure it out.' She insisted.

'So how do I learn to control my dreams then?' asked Brooke.

'I've done some reading up on the ability of lucid dreaming and a lot of different people who have studied the theory give lectures on how to actually use it' said Ricki. 'If we can get you to meet one of them then maybe they can help'.

'Ooh I'm very impressed!' declared Brooke.

Ricki carried on. 'If we can get one of the world's best lecturers on lucid dreaming and get them to teach you how to become in complete control of your dreams then maybe everything else will just fall into place'.

'You make it sound so simple! Joked Brooke.

'Well it's a start' replied Ricki. 'Just don't tell them the real reason behind all this. If you start telling him you've been having psychic premonitions he'll think you're mad and tell you where to go!' she continued.

'Agreed' said Brooke.

Brooke reached out, took Ricki's tablet off the table and began using it.

'I want to get things moving as soon as possible' she said.

'Right, I've already looked up some famous dream lecturers and seen that one lives quite close to us. He's called Dr Barak Gorman' said Ricki, snatching the tablet from Brooke and bringing the man's photo and profile up on screen. He was a middle aged man with receding white hair and a slightly gaunt looking face.

'Great' said Brooke 'I just need to book some kind of one-to-one with him and see if he can help me'. If we can find out where he lives and works I'd like to talk to him personally', she added.

'You might wanna take a shower first!' joked Ricki.

CHAPTER 9

The time was 8.15 AM the following morning. Unaware of exactly when he was going to start his working day Brooke and Ricki were seated on a bench near the entrance to Dr Gorman's office anxiously awaiting his arrival They knew the man was most likely to start his working day at between approximately 8.00AM and 9.00AM. They were sipping cups of coffee and keeping a look out for anyone who might resemble the man they saw in the photo approaching the entrance. They had been there for over 20 minutes and only a small number of people had walked past, none of whom bared any resemblance to the person they were looking for.

The minutes past and the road slowly began to resemble a bustling town centre. More and more people flowed past and more and more cars had gone by. The time had now passed 8.30 AM and several dozen people had wandered past the two sisters at that point. After becoming increasingly bored Ricki decided to buy them both a breakfast meal and another coffee. The time reached

8.45AM and the ladies were finishing their breakfast when someone walking towards the two sisters caught both their attention.

He was a tall gaunt looking man with white hair. He looked like the man in the photograph except that he appeared to have aged somewhat since his profile picture had been taken. Was it an old photograph? In any case they were almost certain it was him. They watched as he approached where they were sitting to see if he was about to enter the door to his office. The sisters gazed in anticipation as the man walked past them and towards the office entrance nearby. It was indeed the man they were looking for.

'That's him', said Brooke as she jumped up out of her seat first and darted towards the man. 'Excuse me' she shouted out to him. 'Excuse me' she shouted again.

Ricki stood up after her sister and started heading slowly towards Brooke and Dr Gorman. The man heard Brooke calling him and turned around to face her.

'Are you Dr Gorman?' Brooke asked.

The man, looking rather surprised and a little bit taken back, replied 'Yes I am'.

'I was wondering if I would be able to talk to you for a moment please?' said Brooke. 'I have studied your work and read your articles on lucid dreaming. I know you're one of the world's top professors on the subject of dreams states and how they can be controlled'.

Dr Gorman looked pleasantly surprised and quite flattered at her remark. He then replied in a slightly modest tone.

'Well I don't know about that but I have certainly spent many years of my life trying to understand the subject. Dreams have always been something that have fascinated me a great deal. For something that forms such a large part of our character and have such an overwhelming impact on our daily lives we know so little about them'.

By this point Brooke had caught up with Dr Gorman and was standing face to face right in front of him. Dr Gorman also noticed Ricki as she strolled up behind Brooke.

'Sorry' she said. Allow me to introduce myself, my name is Brooke and this is my sister Ricki'. They both reached out and shook hands with the Doctor.

'Pleased to meet you both' he replied.

Brooke then continued what she had planned to say before she had introduced herself.

'I would like to know how I too might be able to control my dreams and if you would be willing to teach me. I have recently been having what you might call....vivid dreams in which certain bad things happen. I would obviously be willing to pay you whatever it costs' she added. The doctor stopped and paused for a moment, a little bit unsure of what to say or do.

'If you could spare any time to teach me, or at least give me a chance to try I'd be so grateful. We've travelled all the way across London to see you and we've been sitting here waiting for you for the last hour' added Brooke.

'Well' replied Dr Gorman. 'I think I could spare some time to see you this morning. If I jiggle a few other jobs around then I should be able to fit you in' he added.

The sisters' faces lit up

'Thank you so much that would be wonderful if you could do that!' replied Brooke.

'Let's not stand around in the street any longer. Come inside and sit down while I set up for the day' said Dr Gorman.

'Oh thank you' replied Brooke, with a huge sigh of relief.

Dr Gorman entered his office with the sisters following closely behind.

CHAPTER 10

On the opposite side of his desk the ladies were seated in Dr Gorman's office situated at the end of a short narrow corridor from the front door, lined with drawers and cupboards. The office was somewhat old fashioned in décor. Wooden floors that creaked emphatically upon the contact of footsteps and walls that were touched up in red. Peering around the room they noticed several bookshelves stacked high with reading materials and literature. Pictures of highly different and notably surreal dream states were hung on the walls. One of a seemingly endless staircase leading up to space, one of a car floating towards a distant planet and another one of a house partially submerged in water overlooking the horizon. They all had an eerie yet somewhat tranquil beauty about them. At the far side of the room was a large sofa.

Dr Gorman sat down at his desk after the two young ladies and began in his usual manor. The desk too was old fashioned, crafted from solid oak, sturdy but clearly aged with wear and tear.

On his desk stood an old PC monitor, printer, telephone and paper trays. He opened the top desk drawer on his right hand side and took out a pen and a small writing pad. He jotted down some headings then looked up, directing his attention towards the two sisters, Brooke for the most part.

'So', he said 'Let's begin by hearing about you. First please tell me a bit about yourself. 'How old are you? He asked Brooke.

'Twenty five', she replied.

'Are you married?'

'No' she replied

'What's your occupation?

'I worked as a Market Analyst in the City of London until a few months ago but I'm now technically unemployed' replied Brooke.

'I see, do you live alone or with somebody else' he added.

'I live with my sister' said Brooke nodding her head towards Ricki.

'Interesting' he replied. While asking all these questions Dr Gorman wrote down the answers on his pad.

'Have you recently been through any traumatic incidents in real life, like the death of a close friend or relative or an accident of some kind?' he added.

'No, I haven't had any accidents or lost anyone recently' she replied. 'Losing my job has been the most stressful event of my life this year.' She explained. Ricki remained uncharacteristically silent throughout the whole conversation. She understood the importance of allowing her sister to continue uninterrupted.

'So tell me what happens in these dreams of yours, what do you see?' Dr Gorman asked. Brooke glanced awkwardly over at Ricki and after pondering her response for a few seconds she began.

'I have these really vivid dreams where I see bad things happen to people' she said.

She was all too aware that she couldn't be completely honest with the doctor so she had to twist her story somehow. Glancing over at Ricki again she then continued.

'Well what I'd like is to be able to change these dreams to suit me, to try and change the outcome of them. If the outcome of my dreams can be changed then this will surely help me. If I can change a nightmare into a happy dream then I can make myself happier all round too.' She added.

'Being in control of your dreams is a skill not unlike any other.' Replied Dr Gorman. 'It takes time, practise and patience. It's important not to confuse lucid dreaming with dream control. Lucid dreaming is all about being aware that you're dreaming. Dream control is what follows. It's the ability to consciously and intentionally control what happens in your dreams. With the right training and guidance you'll be able to see things in detail, you'll be able to control, manipulate and even change events that happen but you must understand the distinction before you undertake this task.'

The two ladies sat still in their seats listening to his every word with undivided attention.

'The most important thing to remember first of all is to stay calm and relaxed. As in any situation if you panic then you completely lose your focus and in this case you may even break away from your dreams in a way that might be damaging'.

The doctor started becoming increasingly expressive with his hands as he was explaining.

'The rational side of your brain must be used to its full capacity when dreaming in order to make the right decision about whether you're in a dream state or whether it's real' said Dr Gorman while pointing to his head. 'This is what's known as reality check. Visions we see in our dreams are often blurry, surreal and nonsensical. They often make no sense. Visions in reality on the other hand are very clear and concise. They have continuity and use the physics of space and time. In a dream you might, for instance be suddenly whisked to a faraway country in an instant without any history of how you got there.'

Much like an actor the doctor pronounced all his words in their entirety and spoke very clearly and concisely. His accent was that of Received Pronunciation and therefore undetectable of where he came from. He then continued.

'The rational part of your brain in real life will tell you that in order to get there you would need to go through the motions of travelling to an airport, then boarding a plane and flying there which could take several hours or even days. It's making this distinction while you are dreaming that is essential to knowing that you are in fact in a dream and being able to control your dream. You have to look for the tell-tale signs while you are dreaming. If something isn't right, if something doesn't make sense then you have to challenge it and say to yourself "What am I doing here?"'

Dr Gorman paused for a moment and took a breath. He reached over to his tray and grabbed a leaflet which he handed to Brooke.

'I hope I haven't bombarded you with too much information!' he joked. 'If you'd like to come and visit me again for a full session then I'd like to set you a kind of homework assignment to do beforehand. I want you to try and attempt your own reality check and be able to acknowledge your dreams when you are sleeping. Let your rational mind tell you when you're in a dream state. Once you have done this then you'll have achieved the first step in controlling your dreams. Perhaps even try and control your own actions' he added. 'But remember to start off small, try doing some simple mundane things like walking and turning'

'You'll need at least a few days' he insisted. 'How about I fit you in on Friday at 10.30AM?' he asked.

'That's fine by me', replied Brooke.

'Another thing' he added. 'I'd like to carry out some tests and with your permission I'd like to inject you with a mild sedative that will hopefully put you to sleep for an hour or so, just long enough for me to help start you off on your dream control' he asked.

'Errr....OK' replied Brooke looking somewhat apprehensive.

She took the leaflet then the two sisters thanked the doctor for his time, walked out the office and headed home.

CHAPTER 11

Brooke had read the entirety of the leaflet Dr Gorman gave her before she had even left his office. The document essentially paraphrased most of what the doctor had said to her. Nonetheless she studied it again and again every night before she went to bed and would re-site certain sections of it.

The next few hours Brooke spent remembering what the doctor had said and discussing her thoughts and feelings with Ricki.

'Look for the tell-tale signs' she said. 'Stay calm and relaxed, what am I doing here? Does this all make sense?'

After tucking under the sheets she dropped in to her pillow and persevered with her recitals. She then slowly began to drop off.

While sleeping she fell in to another dream state. Blurry images appeared. It felt so real. There were noises...footsteps walking...up steps...down steps...automatic doors opening and closing... voices echoing over a loudspeaker...a train pulled away. She was at the railway station. The train disappeared to reveal a lonely woman left behind by the rest of the passengers who shot passed her with indifference at how slowly she was moving. The lady seemed distressed, in pain, her movement stalled to an almost complete stop. She moved her hand to her chest. Her face appeared increasingly twisted and concerned. She fell to the ground unnoticed. All the other passengers had their backs turned and were making their way out at pace. Brooke could see everything happening but was unaware that she was dreaming. To her it was almost like she was watching a movie.

She continued to dream and have visions, yet each one was indistinguishable from reality for her. When she saw these visions she was still unaware that it was a dream. Her attempt at reality check had failed. She awoke the next morning and instantly felt the agonising disappointment of her defeat.

She rose from bed with a certain air of weariness at her situation. She was fighting a battle and was currently on the losing side. Her attempts to overcome her problem had proved futile and she had never taken well to losing.

She left the bedroom and strolled into the kitchen, her proverbial tail between her legs. She made herself a large, strong cup of coffee and sat down at the table. She quickly buried herself in her thoughts and sat there in an almost dreamlike daze, staring at her coffee cup.

Ricki then strolled in quite casually.

'Morning' she uttered. Brooke was startled by the sudden disturbance and looked up, in awe at first then quickly relaxing after the initial shock.

'Ohh, good morning' she replied.

'How did it go last night?' asked Ricki while pouring out some coffee that Brooke had made.

Talking understatedly Brooke replied.

'It didn't quite go as I wanted it to.' I had visions like I've had before but I still wasn't able to change anything. I could quite clearly see everything but it was like I was still a spectator'.

Once again Ricki endeavoured to give words of encouragement and support.

'Well it's only been one night' she insisted. 'Like the doctor said it takes time and practise. Don't give up so easily'.

'But I tried so hard to do it' replied Brooke defiantly. 'I don't know how to change my thoughts while I'm dreaming' she added.

'I'm sure you will somehow', insisted Ricki. 'I know you'll figure this out, you always do' she said.

'But I've never had to face anything like this before' replied Brooke. 'It's all completely new to me' she insisted. This is like nothing that I have ever s...'

Interrupting her Ricki spoke up. 'This is not like you to be so negative' she continued now raising her voice. 'I know you can overcome this and more. You've always won everything. You always overcome the odds and find a way to succeed. You have never failed at anything in your life. You don't know how to fail!'

Brooke was left bamboozled by what Ricki said. She knew her younger sister was right and this gave her some re-assurance.

'Look why don't I try and help you?' added Ricki. 'The next time you fall asleep I can try and talk to you while you're dreaming. They say that you can still hear while you're asleep so why don't we try that? She continued.

'Yes that's a good idea' replied Brooke. 'If you're OK with me falling asleep and you staying awake for once!?' she joked.

'Ha ha ha very funny!' replied Ricki rather sarcastically.

CHAPTER 12

That night Brooke was preparing for bed to try and fall asleep alongside her sister. Ricki had arranged her chair to sit right next to her while she was dreaming and had made herself a strong cup of coffee that she left on Brooke's bedside table. From here she was able to speak to Brooke and act as her guide while she slept. Brooke on the other hand had prepared herself by taking a sleeping pill several minutes previously to ensure that her slumber was well in advance of her sister's.

'Right' said Brooke while climbing into bed, pulling the sheets over herself and lying down on her back. 'I'm gonna try and fall asleep now but remember it could be several minutes or even hours before I start dreaming. Keep a look out for the tell-tale signs from your end. It's likely that my breathing patterns will change and become slower and deeper. That's when I need you to start speaking to me. Speak softly but just loud enough that I can hear you, but not too loud that you'll startle me and wake me up.'

'What exactly should I say to you?' asked Ricki.

'Like we went through earlier' Brooke replied. 'I need you to re-assure me. Just keep telling me that I'm dreaming and that I'm actually asleep in bed with you sitting next to me' She replied. 'I should be able to hear everything you say so hopefully I'll be aware of what's really happening' she added.

Brooke reached over and switched off her bedside light then rested her head back into her pillow. The room was saved from complete darkness by a dim reflection of light coming from the hallway outside. It was just enough for Ricki to see her sister but dark enough not to be a disturbance. She shut her eyes and tried to relax herself.

'Sweet dreams!' joked Ricki leaning over the bed.

Brooke then re-opened one eye aimed at Ricki with a kind of bemused shock.

'Fat chance!' she exclaimed.

The two of them then laughed out loud together. Ricki chuckled so hard that she leaned out and fell backwards on her chair. The momentum was so fast that the chair fell beyond its centre of gravity. Before Ricki had time to react she and the back end of the chair hit the floor with a thud. Brooke now lying in her bed with both eyes open saw it all happen and laughed out loud all the more hysterically. This was the funniest thing she had seen in weeks. Ricki laid down with her back to the floor and her feet still in the air. Brooke didn't bother doing anything to help her sister. She couldn't even if she wanted to. She was paralysed with uncontrollable laughter.

Still in shock, Ricki lay on the floor for several seconds before she could fully comprehend what had happened. She then slowly nudged onto her side and proceeded to rise to her feet with a mixed feeling of shock and amusement. Brooke continued to chuckle relentlessly. It's like this whole experience had acted like a release valve for all the pressure she had built up over the last few days. Now the pressure was being let out.

'Ha ha ha, very funny, I'm glad someone's happy!' Ricki declared sarcastically as she stood up with Brooke continuing to laugh out loud.

Several minutes passed by and Brooke slowly began to calm down and relax. Ricki waited patiently as Brooke lay back down and nestled her head on her pillow once more. The sisters were now taking the moment seriously. The room was filled with a peaceful silence as Ricki watched over her sister lying in front of her. Brooke's eyes closed shut and her body laid still. She became increasingly comfortable and soon forgot all about her sister's recent little slapstick incident. Ricki continued to watch over her as she slowly began to fall fast asleep.

CHAPTER 13

Several more minutes passed. By now Ricki had impatiently finished her coffee and was becoming increasingly bored sitting there with nothing to do. She began to fidget and move about in her chair as she observed her sister. She was unsure about when exactly she would make contact with Brooke and became somewhat anxious. Her sister remained silently asleep for the whole time, her breathing barely making a sound.

After a short time her breaths very slowly, and almost without being noticeable, became gradually deeper and deeper. Brooke's lungs slowly began filling up with more and more air. As she inhaled her chest began to tighten in deeper then rise higher as her lungs expelled the air out. The noise of her breathing became increasingly apparent. As she lay still in her bed the look on her face began to change very slightly. Inside Brooke's head something was starting to happen.

Ricki acknowledged the changes in her sister's activity. Waiting for Brooke to become properly engaged by her sleep she remained seated silently.

She decided against speaking at this time and risk startling her sister until her sleep became deeper. She waited a short time longer still. By this time Brooke's heavier breathing had become ever more prominent. Ricki noticed Brooke's eyes flickering as if they were blinking but without opening.

Ricki decided it was now the right time to engage with her sister as she slept.

'Brooke?' she whispered to her softly. Unresponsive, Brooke remained fast asleep and stayed absolutely still.

'Brooke?' she whispered again. Brooke once again remained unresponsive.

'Brooke' she said again for a third time. 'It's me Ricki' she said. 'I know you can hear me, you're in bed asleep and I'm sitting next to you, you're dreaming and I'm here to help you...'

CHAPTER 14

Dark Blurry lines appeared. Shadowy textures were seen. Brooke found herself in another strange place. Where was this place? It wasn't like most other dreams of hers. It was quiet and peaceful. There were no cars or traffic nearby. No pedestrians walking past. Only trees, plants, grass and hedgerows. No noises could be heard from anything. Even the wind stayed away. It was an idyllic setting. Lush green vegetation stretched as far as the eye could see. A narrow footpath that ran through the scenery was the closest there was to a trace of human life.

The tranquillity of the location was interrupted by a very faint call. She heard the word 'Brooke' being called out in the distance. What could it be? She listened out for more distant sounds. Again she heard the word 'Brooke', only this time a little louder and clearer. Confusion ensued. Who was this who was calling her name and why? She heard her name being called again for a third time. 'Brooke, it's me Ricki, I know you can hear me, you're in bed asleep and I'm sitting next to you,

you're dreaming and I'm here to help you.'

The voice of her sister made Brooke feel some-what bizarre. She had never had a sensation like this before. She didn't know how to react at first. Her sister then continued to speak to her.

'You need to try and stay in this dream state while I talk to you. Remember you need to stay calm and relaxed and focused. Take in all your surround-ings. Whatever it is you're seeing you're not really there. Remember what the doctor said, you gotta think about this rationally' said Ricki.

Brooke then began to feel re-assured by her sister's voice. She trusted her words and began to under-stand her own situation. She had come to the real-isation that she was indeed dreaming. Ricki con-tinued to speak to her as she slept.

'Only you can see what's happening so I have to as-sume that you're dreaming right now and that you can hear me while you're sleeping.' said Ricki with her voice remaining soft and silent. She remem-bered that the slightest increase in noise could jolt her sister into waking up.

'The first thing you have to do is be able to see yourself, make yourself physical. You need to give yourself a body, your body. Look down at your hands and feet.' Ricki whispered.

Something unusual happened to Brooke. A strange sensation came over her. It was like she felt herself come alive. She now had a body, of sorts. She became an entity in her own dream state. She responded to what Ricki said and looked down at her hands and feet. Her feet were bare and she was wearing her nightgown. The one she had worn to bed.

'Now touch your face' Ricki continued. Brooke did as Ricki told her and ran her fingers gently across her own face'. It felt almost real. 'I don't know if you can see me but if it's easier then just imagine me and I'll appear'. Brooke responded. She turned around to see her sister right there in front of her. At least it looked just like Ricki. She was standing facing her, straight faced. It wasn't her obviously, just Brooke's manifestation of Ricki in casual clothes, as Brooke had last remembered her.

As Ricki spoke to her in real life, so too did her manifestation in the dream. 'I'll assume that you can see me now?' said the manifestation.

This was too much for Brooke to take. She found it all to be quite disturbing. How was she able to do this so vividly?

CHAPTER 15

Brooke lay absolutely still in bed with Ricki still at her side. All of a sudden she sat up sharply and opened her eyes. She was breathing franticly, like she had woken from a horrible nightmare, as was often the case with her recently. She sat facing directly in front of her still panting.

Ricki was completely startled. She gasped. Like someone had jump scared her from behind. 'Oh my god, you scared the crap out of me!' she said to Brooke.

'That was so weird!' panted Brooke, still trying to keep her breathing under control. 'It was too much for me to take, it was just so freaky seeing you like that, it was like you were there with me.'

'You saw me!?' asked Ricki with great excitement.

'Yeah' said Brooke.

'Did you hear me too?' she asked. Brooke nodded as she turned to face her, now with her breathing more under control and feeling much more relaxed.

'Wow! That's exciting!!' she exclaimed. 'What happened then, what made you wake up?' she added.

'You did' replied Brooke. 'It was all a bit too much for me to take. I knew where I was. When I saw you speak to me it was kinda freaky!'

'I only spoke to you for a short time, about a minute at the most' said Ricki. 'It seemed like longer than that' said Brooke. 'Did I talk back to you at all in that time?'

'No' replied Ricki. 'You barely even moved'. Now much more relaxed with her breathing and heart rate returning to normal Brooke lay back on her bed and rested her head on the pillow.

'At least we made some progress tonight. This is something we can tell the doctor when we see him' added Ricki.

'Yeah that's true' replied Brooke 'But I've done enough for tonight. I just wanna lie here and relax for now if that's OK.' She said rhetorically.

In response Ricki stood up out of the chair.

'OK. I don't think I'm gonna sleep anytime soon after drinking that coffee. I think I'll go and watch some crappy film on TV'.

She bent over and kissed Brooke on the forehead then picked up the chair and walked out.

'Good night' she said as the door closed behind

her.

'Good night' replied Brooke.

CHAPTER 16

The following morning Brooke was sitting in the kitchen listening to the radio. Something she enjoyed doing but hadn't done recently. She was content with listening to her favourite station playing Indie and alternative rock music. The window blinds were open and the room was glowing from the daylight pouring in. Drinking her freshly brewed coffee she sat there feeling somewhat relaxed. Her emotions were now filled with a glow of optimism rather than fear and dread. There was hope for her to succeed and she could feel it now. She had a plan for the first time. A clearer vision of what she was going to do. She remained still in her chair, deep in thoughts that made her grow with excitement. She had a challenge ahead of her of course, but she now knew how to face it.

Ricki walked in still wearing her nightdress, rubbing her eyes to adjust to the brightness of the room. 'Morning' she said.

'Good morning' replied Brooke.

'How you feelin'?' asked Ricki.

'Better, thanks.' She replied. 'I slept better last night than I have for a while now. I've also got a better idea of what to do now' she added.

'Good. That's nice to know' replied Ricki while pouring herself some coffee and sitting down next to Brooke.

'D'you wanna go through what we did again last night?' she asked Brooke.

'Yes. I think I do' replied Brooke with re-assurance. 'I know what I did wrong last night. This time I won't panic. I'll be more in control and I'll know what to do.' She added.

Brooke's response made Ricki feel a lot happier and her positivity was rubbing off on her. She now felt a lot more re-assured by the way her sister was acting.

'Do you still need me to sit and talk to you as you sleep?' she asked.

'Yeah I think so', replied Brooke. 'I think soon enough I'll be able to figure it out by myself though. I have to. I can't have you sitting over me like you did last night forever now can I!?' She added.

'I guess not' replied Ricki.

The sisters spent much of the rest of the day re-laxing in each other's company. They watched movies, played video games and enjoyed a bottle of wine together with their dinner. They were sisters again. Friends like they always used to be. They both forgot just how much they enjoyed the other ones company. They decided to play their favourite board game together. The 'Impersonating Game'

With help from her sister Ricki had previously designed and invented her own board game in which you select a card with a friend or celebrity's name on then have to impersonate that individual. She had even crafted her own board from an old piece of card. The rules were simple. Each player started at the beginning of the board, rolled the dice and moved that many spaces to a square. Each square was colour coded to represent a different category of individual to impersonate. There were six categories of people. They were personal acquaintances and friends, actors and entertainers, sports stars and athletes, Politicians, historical figures and fictional characters. The player then had to pick the correct colour card from the top of the pile and attempt to impersonate whoever's name was on the card. If the impression made any of the other players laugh – regardless of how good or bad it was, or if the impression was deemed to be convincing enough then that player got to roll again and move further around the board. If the impression was bad or if the player forfeited they either had to go back ten spaces or down a shot of spirits. Bringing alcohol into the game obviously made it more interesting.

The winner was the first one to reach the end space and do one final impression of whoever the player on their left had selected. If the impression was successful they won the game. If not they had to down a shot, wait until their next turn and try someone else.

Common people that they wrote on the cards to impersonate were a very mixed bag including Michael Caine, Frank Spencer, Marilyn Monroe, Janet Street Porter, Sean Connery, Cilla Black, Arnold Schwarzenegger, David Bowie, Sylvester Stallone, Adolf Hitler, Dolly Parton, Jack Nicholson, Ariana Grande, Robert De Niro, Cher, Al Pacino, Liam Gallagher, Britney Spears, Kermit the Frog, Miss Piggy, William Shakespeare, Robin Hood, Batman and Basil Fawlty.

The game was obviously better with more players but since only the two of them were around they had to suffice. Their impressions were mostly terrible, but at least they made each other laugh.

CHAPTER 17

The day passed by so quickly and before long the sisters found themselves in the same place they were the night before, Brooke lying in bed and Ricki by her side watching over her with a strong, even stronger cup of coffee. Both ladies began to relax. No longer active, and with alcohol still in their systems the drinks began to have a calming effect on the two of them, particularly Brooke. Before lying down to rest Brooke began to go through the plan yet again.

'OK' she said 'When I fall asleep you need to wait for the tell-tale signs again' she added. 'As before my breathing will change, my body and mind will become more submerged and that's when I'll start dreaming. At that point you need to try and speak to me again. Just try not to startle me this time'.

'You try not to panic!' insisted Ricki.

'OK, OK I'll try' replied Brooke. 'Just remember to keep your voice at the right level' she added.

Brooke laid her head back and closed her eyes. Calm and relaxed she lay still. With eyelids shut she was quickly in the early stages of falling asleep, this time much faster than last night. Was it the alcohol? Or perhaps it was due to a less anxious state of mind, or both. Ricki looked on as her sister fell into her slumber, watching her every breath with complete anticipation.

Several minutes passed and Ricki began to acknowledge Brooke's change in sleep patterns. Identically to the night before, only this time all the more quickly. Her breathing changed, her chest expansions and contractions became increasingly more apparent. The noise of air escaping her lungs became more distinctive. Ricki was now more confident in knowing when to engage.

'Brooke?' said Ricki quite softly. Her sister remained still and unresponsive. 'Brooke?' she said again. 'It's Ricki'.

CHAPTER 18

Dark Blurry lines appeared. Shadowy textures were seen. Brooke found herself in another strange place. Where was this place? It wasn't like most other dreams of hers. It was quiet and peaceful. There were no cars or traffic nearby. No pedestrians walking past. Only trees, plants, grass and hedgerows. No noises could be heard from anything. Even the wind stayed away. It was an idyllic setting. Lush green vegetation stretched as far as the eye could see. A narrow footpath that ran through the scenery was the closest there was to a trace of human life. But wait. This was all too familiar. She felt a huge sensation of déjà vu. Something wasn't right. She couldn't quite comprehend her predicament.

Suddenly a familiar voice echoed in the distance.

'Brooke'. The voice drew her attention. Who was this calling her name, and why? The voice sounded all too familiar. She listened tentatively for the voice again. 'Brooke' she heard, only much louder and clearer this time.

'It's Ricki'.

At that point Brooke suddenly realised everything. She knew she was dreaming. She looked down at her hands and feet. She was once again wearing the nightgown she had put on before bed. She turned around and saw Ricki's manifestation again, as large as life she appeared just inches in front of her. This time keeping calm, she saw and heard her sister talk.

'Brooke you're dreaming again' she said.

'No shit!' said Brooke standing face to face with her sister.

'I see you' she said to Ricki. 'This is where I was last night' she added. Ricki's manifestation gazed back at her.

'If you're talking to me I can't hear you but I'm assuming you can see and hear me' she said.

'If you can hear me then let's start by performing some simple actions' she continued. 'You have to quite literally walk before you can run. Firstly try and imagine me walking away from you'. She added.

Then just as sure as she said Ricki slowly began to walk backwards away from her, one step at a time. She walked, just a few footsteps then continued.

'Now just imagine yourself walking towards me'.

Brooke acknowledged her sister's instructions and responded. She slowly lifted her right knee and delicately put her foot forward. Her foot sank down and landed gently on the ground, no sound was made. Joyfully happy at the progress of what would seem like such a simple task she tried the same with her left leg. This time with more confidence she almost effortlessly raised her left knee, put her foot forward and rested it on the ground. She had now taken two footsteps and had the confidence to move quicker, and with less concentration. She put her right knee up again, put her foot forward and rested it on the ground. Then put her left knee up again, foot forward then to ground. She had taken four steps and by now it had become second nature. She took two more steps with ease and caught up with Ricki. The two of them stood facing each other.

'I'm assuming that you managed that?' said Ricki. 'Now try and hold out your hand to touch mine' she said as her apparition put her hand out in front of her.

Brooke responded by holding out her hand and touching her sister's.

'Stroke it, feel it, run your fingers along the palms and feel the lines, feel the skin, feel the bones around my knuckles and fingers.' Ricki added.

Brooke did as she instructed. She felt Ricki's hand and stroked it. She ran her fingers across her palm and felt all sensations like it was real. Her hand was soft, like her own. The lines on her palms were defined but smooth. She felt the warmth of her skin radiate through to her own. How could this be a dream? It felt so real, she thought to her herself.

'Let's turn your attention away from me now' said Ricki. 'Now look all around you and take in your surroundings. Look down at the ground and up to the sky. Look in all directions, high and low. What do you see in the distance? Trees, plants, build-ings, birds. Take it all in'.

Brooke once again reacted to her sister's instruc-tions in a way that was beyond anything she had felt before. Everything became clear to her. She looked all around herself, high and low. She could not only see the trees and the landscape and the buildings, but she could hear it all too. She heard the birds flapping their wings as they flew around in the sky, the gentle wind howling, the insects in the grass. The scent of flowers became so strong it almost overpowered her. Her senses had become amplified.

'You see the birds in the distance, now see them flying towards you, closer and closer.' Said Ricki. 'They are gliding around the sky over you.... now imagine one of them shitting on you!!' she joked.

Sure enough one of the birds in her dream did in-deed poop on her from high up in the sky. The mess fell down from high, landed on her head and splatted all through her hair.

All of a sudden Brooke yelled out in horror and

sat up from her bed. The trauma and surprise of her sister's practical joke caused her to wake up in a panic. She gently touched her head on top to feel for anything. There was nothing but her own clean, unsoiled hair. It was a dream.

Of course the whole ordeal made Ricki roar with laughter. As far as she was concerned she had just been sitting by her sister's bed watching her sleep.

'Wow! You actually fell for that!' she laughed. 'I can't believe you fell for that!' Brooke was now wide awake and clearly quite stunned and appalled at her sister.

'You weren't supposed to shock me like that!' she insisted.

'I couldn't help it' answered Ricki. 'So you really got shat on in your dream!?' she asked.

'Yes of course' replied Brooke 'I did everything you said, I walked towards you, held your hand, then looked at my surroundings just like you told me to'.

'And saw the birds above you too!?' asked Ricki.

'Yes' replied Brooke 'It all felt so real to me, my senses became a lot stronger, I could see and hear everything like never before'.

'We made good progress then didn't we?' said Ricki

'Yes but I think I've done enough for one night' replied Brooke. 'If it's OK I'm gonna rest again for a bit' she added.

Brooke then sank her head back on to her pillow once again and began to calm herself down.

CHAPTER 19

The next morning Brooke woke up earlier than Ricki, as was usually the case, and decided to relax in the living room to eat her breakfast. She turned on the TV, and avoiding all chance of seeing any news, flicked over to a music channel. She sat in the living room eagerly awaiting her sister to come and join her. She had just one day left before she had to see Dr Gorman and was excited about what she wanted to try and do again tonight.

'Morning' said Ricki as she strolled in casually with her cup of coffee sitting down next to Brooke.

'So glad you could join me!' said Brooke with a certain air of smugness. 'I really think I'm getting the hang of this now' she continued. 'Last night was another break-through for me, despite your stupid antics! I think I am well on the way to mastering this newly found skill of mine. I'm actually looking forward to hitting the sack tonight. I know exactly what I need to do, I can't hold back at all this time.'

'So far you've managed to do simple things like

turning your head, walking and holding things in your hand, right?' asked Ricki with Brooke nodding as her sister spoke. 'Well why don't we try some more challenging activities' she continued. 'We could try you with running for example?'

'Yes' replied Brooke 'Although you'd certainly be much better at that than me! she joked 'You were always much faster than I ever was'

'Well if you're in a dream then I guess you can be as fast as you like' replied Ricki after pausing for a moment. 'You're right though, I was much faster than you ever were. It was the only thing I could ever do better than you!' she added.

'That and hide and seek' insisted Brooke. 'I could never figure out where you hid in the house. Where was your secret hiding place' she added.

'That's a secret!' replied Ricki insistently. 'So do you want me around again tonight?' she asked.

'Yeah' replied Brooke. 'If you could sit with me and talk me through it again, and if you could NOT pull any more stupid pranks that would be appreciated too!'

Ricki chuckled in response to her sister. 'That was so funny' she laughed. 'The way you flew up out of the bed in horror, I laughed so much I nearly threw up'.

'Well I'm glad you thought it was so funny but to me it seemed so real' insisted Brooke looking somewhat annoyed.

'I think Dr Gorman's gonna be very impressed with you' said Ricki 'I wonder what exactly he'll have in store for ya. Do you think we should tell him the truth about your dreams at any time?' she asked.

'No definitely not' insisted Brooke. 'We need to keep this strictly between ourselves, certainly for now at least' she added.

'OK' said Ricki nodding in agreement. 'What do you wanna do today?' she asked 'Fancy a race to the shopping mall for some retail therapy? The exercise will help you sleep better'

Disapproving with her sister's suggestion Brooke looked at Ricki with a serious face then before she spoke, thought about what she said, then hesitated. 'Yeah alright then' she replied.

The two sisters finished their breakfast, got dressed then headed out. They arrived back several hours later with carrier bags full of clothes, jewellery and a large takeaway dinner. Ricki convinced Brooke that they needed a lot of food with the excuse that a big meal would help her sleep better. They threw down their bags and sat in the kitchen eating their newly bought feast.

CHAPTER 20

That night the two sisters found themselves in the same place for the third time in a row - Brooke lying in bed with Ricki at her side.

'Right remember what we discussed again' said Brooke. 'You need to encourage me to run and jump and do lots of different things this time, OK? The more physical the better but this time, no more stupid practical jokes!' she added

'OK' smirked Ricki. Brooke then rested her head back, closed her eyes and slowly drifted into sleep.

Before long she was fast asleep, back in her place. It was quiet and peaceful, no cars or traffic. No pedestrians. No noise, just trees and plants. She knew where she was right away. She heard Ricki's voice in the distance 'Brooke', 'Brooke' she said, before her apparition appeared. 'You're dreaming again' said Ricki.

'I know' replied Brooke.

'I'm assuming you can see and hear me again' said Ricki. 'Remember I can't hear you so you'll just have to do what I say' she added. 'Let's start with you moving towards me and taking my hand like last time.'

Brooke once again followed her sister's instructions and walked towards her. She took Ricki's hand in hers as she did the night before. She felt the soft touch of her palms and the warmth of her skin. It felt so real yet she knew that it wasn't.

'Now let's try moving on a bit and doing something a bit more physical' said Ricki. 'You said there's a narrow pathway leading through this place, so follow it and try to run along it'

Brooke obeyed her sister's instructions and found herself along the pathway in her dream. She started to stroll then slowly built up speed. Her stroll turned into a walk, her walk turned to pacing, and then her pacing turned to speed-walking. She was moving at a rapid pace just one notch short of running. She thought about running, how and if she could do it. Was she able to do it? What would happen if she started running? Would she fall over? Where would it take her? All these questions and more went through her head as she moved along the footpath.

Then she thought to herself, why worry? This was only a dream after all and she was the one in control of herself. She set her mind free from fear and disbelief then began her endeavour to move up a notch. She started to move her feet faster.

Her arms changed position and began to move in rhythm with her legs. The surrounding grass and vegetation began to move past her at a higher rate. Her hair blew in the wind. Her fast walk had turned into a slow jog. She carried on at a steady speed then heard her sister's voice.

'Run! See just how fast you can go!' said Ricki.

Brooke acknowledged her sister's advice once again. She moved her feet ever more quickly and her arms continued in rhythm with her legs. Her slow jog had turned into a run. The noise of the dirt and gravel along the footpath became more defined, the grinding and crunching of the stones and pebbles as her feet hit the ground more apparent. She was enjoying this. It was like running a marathon without getting exhausted, having all of the good and none of the bad.

Not content with remaining at her current speed she decided to up her game. She wanted to see just how fast she could really go. She began to move her legs faster still. Her run turned into a sprint. She ran as fast as she had ever run in her life. She hadn't run this fast since she had been a teenager at school. She hadn't needed to.

'See if you can go faster still' said Ricki

Still intent on taking it further Brooke decided she was going to go beyond the threshold of what she could ever possibly be capable of in the real world. She accelerated her speed further still. Her legs moved faster and faster. The air began to howl past her face. She ran like the wind, the speed of a world class sprinter.

She accelerated faster and faster still. Her movement was so fast that the surrounding grass and vegetation became little more than a blur. She hit super-human speed. Way beyond what any real woman or man could possibly achieve. The speed was pure adrenaline rush. Her facial expression changed from serious to a beaming grin. She was loving it. Like a comic book hero who had just discovered their powers for the first time. She felt almost invincible.

'Keep a look out for any obstacles, you don't want to fall over!' uttered a familiar voice. With that a large wooden gate appeared in front of her. It was Brooke's un-conscience reaction to her sister's advice. The gate was over four feet high and drew close to Brooke very quickly, but she was now completely un-phased. She jumped high in the air and cleared the gate with ease. She landed on the opposite side and continued to sprint. She turned around laughing to see the gate become smaller and smaller in the distance behind her until it was nothing but a tiny dot.

She turned back to face the front pondering to herself. How could she possibly jump like that? She had never made anything that high in her life. She wanted to push herself further with this still.

She decided to make another gate appear as she was running. Sure enough the gate appeared, this time twice as big as the one before. She approached the gate in almost no time and leapt right over in a single bound, effortlessly. She hit the ground running once again and without any loss of momentum she continued to storm ahead. Like the previous jump she turned around to see the gate disappear in the distance behind her, laughing more.

This is absolutely amazing! She thought to herself. This was one of the greatest moments of her life. It wasn't real but she didn't care. To her at that moment it felt indistinguishable from reality.

She continued to sprint for some time until the excitement became all too much for her. She had to stop running and collect her thoughts in the dream while she was still able to. She gradually started to slow down her pace. Her super-human speed slowly reduced to that of a world class athlete. From there she slowly toned it down to the speed of her sprinting, to running then to jogging. She eventually grinded to a halt and stood still.

Brooke looked all around herself. She seemed to be in exactly the same place where she had started. Surrounded by plants and vegetation she could still see the trees in the distance with the birds flying in circles. She had run so fast and covered such a long distance, many miles in total, yet she had gone nowhere. That's how dreams are.

They don't need to make sense after all. Nonetheless she felt happy and exhilarated, delighted with what she had achieved.

Brooke felt an irresistible urge to return to the real world and tell her sister everything. She decided to wake herself up. At this time she only needed to want to wake up and it would happen. Her vision turned into a blur and noises became distant. Her consciousness was slowly being transferred back to reality. She was pulling herself back into the real world.

Lying in bed, her eyes opened wide. Brooke sat up sharply.

'Wow that was amazing!!' she screamed out loud.

She received no reaction from her outburst. Glancing to her left she saw Ricki seated in the chair, her head tilted to the side and her eyes closed. She had nodded off in that time. Brooke chuckled at the site of her sister asleep and silently sank back into her pillow beaming with delight.

CHAPTER 21

The next morning the two sisters made their way to Dr Gorman's office again. They arrived on time and went straight in to see him. Sitting on the opposite side of his desk the doctor began to speak to the two of them.

'So welcome back to my office again. Do you have any news since we last spoke? Have you been practising like I asked?'

The sisters glanced at each other with a slightly awkward grin. Brooke then spoke.

'Well... yes you could say that' she replied. 'I've made a lot of progress over the last few days with the help of my sister. I've been consciously active in my dreams. I would go to bed with Ricki sitting at my side to watch me while I sleep and help direct me when I'm dreaming. She appeared in my dreams whenever she spoke to me. We started with simple tasks like turning, walking, and holding things. Then by the time I fell asleep last night I could run like the wind. I felt myself move like lightning through the fields, jumping over gates, going faster and faster. There were no limits to how fast I could go and I have to say it was amazing!' insisted Brooke.

'My goodness, you have made progress haven't you?' replied Dr Gorman. 'I've been taking time to think more about your situation and I'd very much like to run some additional tests on you if I can?' he added

'OK' replied Brooke. 'What is it exactly that you wanted to try?' she asked

'I have planned a series of psychometric and cognitive tests that will help me understand your brain functionality. The tests consist of a range of analytical, practical and creative skill questions both individually and intertwined. The outcome will also help you to understand yourself better. Have you ever taken an IQ test?' he asked

'No' replied Brooke looking at Ricki.

'Why does she need an IQ test?' asked Ricki.

'I'd like to know and understand your intellect further. This will allow me to fully comprehend your mind. I know you're a very clever young lady but I'd like to know just how intelligent you really are and what aspects of your intellect stand out the most. This will help me to help you. I'd like to put you through The Wechsler Adult Intelligence Scale test. It's one of the most widely used and accurate IQ measuring tools. The combination of brain volume, speed of variability in the neural transmission in your brain, and its working memory capacity are all related to IQ. The more variable a brain i.e. the more its different parts frequently connect with each other, the higher a person's IQ and creativity are.'

Barely comprehending a word the doctor just said Ricki glanced at Brooke with an awkward look of confusion. 'Did you understand that!?' she asked her, quite worryingly.

'More or less' replied Brooke.

Dr Gorman continued 'Recent research has just confirmed something I already knew in that there is a high correlation between lucid dreaming and problem-solving abilities. In other words the more intelligent you are the more vivid your dreaming is, and the more vivid your dreams are the more intelligent you are.'

'Prepare to be amazed!' said Ricki smiling at them both. 'Brooke is the cleverest person I've ever known!' she added.

The doctor continued 'One of the most interesting questions raised is whether high insight causes lucid dreaming, lucid dreaming causes an increase in insight, or a third, as yet unidentified variable causes an increase in both lucid dreaming and insight. It is my own personal belief that all three reasons are equally responsible for the other two. I hope you're not in any rush today as this may take a few hours' said the doctor.

Addressing Ricki he added 'At the risk of sounding rather rude I'm afraid I must ask you to wait outside while your sister and I run through the IQ test. I hope you understand but I cannot risk having any interference of any kind while I run through these tests.' he continued.

Ricki acknowledge the doctor's request and proceeded to exit the room. 'I'll go for a walk around the town' she said as she walked out.

'OK Thanks, I'll call you when I'm done' replied Brooke.

CHAPTER 22

Brooke remained in her chair as the doctor reached down and grabbed a file from one of his bottom drawers. He reached down again and produced a stop watch and an old fashioned tape recorder which he placed at the side of his table. 'I have prepared a series of suitable questions that will test virtually every aspect of your mental capabilities' he said. 'The questions will also be tape recorded and timed. Let's start with some relatively easy questions just to warm up' he added

'Are you ready?' he asked Brooke

'Yes' she replied

'Good, then let's begin' said the doctor as he reached over and started the tape recorder and timer.

'First question, - I am a drink. I am also a letter of the alphabet? What am I?'

'Tea' replied Brooke without even hesitating.

'Good' said the doctor. 'Next question - I have a

tongue but I can't talk. I have no legs or wings but I can move from one place to another. What am I?'

'A shoe' she replied, once again without hesitation.

'Very good' said the doctor. 'Next question – 'If a woman and a half can eat a hamburger and a half in a minute and a half, how long would it take six women to eat six hamburgers?'

'A minute' she replied still without hesitation.

'I can fill up an entire room and still not take up any space. What am I?'

'A light' she replied

The doctor smiled at her in approval. 'I can see these questions have all been a little bit easy. Now we move on to the more difficult brain teasers' He added.

'Exactly how much soil is there in a hole that's six metres by four metres by four metres?'

'If it's a hole then there can't be any soil so there is none' said Brooke

'Excellent' he replied

'The ages of a father and his graduate daughter add up to 66. The father's age is the two digits of his daughter's age reversed. How old are they?'

'If she's a graduate then it's most likely 24 and 42 which means there's only eighteen years difference in their age.' replied Brooke instantaneously. 'They could theoretically be 15 and 51, although 15 would be an extremely young age to have a degree.' said Brooke

The doctor continued with his questions. 'Seven people meet up for a party. Each person at the party shakes hands with each other person just once. How many handshakes have taken place at the party?'

'Twenty One' replied Brooke.

Astounded at the speed and confidence of her responses the doctor looked on with amazement. He continued to ask her a series of questions, all of which she answered with little or no thought process. He was so amazed at her that he began to doubt the integrity of the test.

'You haven't somehow seen these questions before have you?' he asked.

'No' replied Brooke with total conviction.

Studying her response he found no evidence in her body language that gave away any dishonesty. He knew when someone was lying to him yet with Brooke there was nothing that looked out of place. He continued the IQ test with further questions, each one more intellectually challenging than the last. Challenging that is for other people who have sat the tests. For Brooke every question was answered correctly and with great speed. He then asked her to sit through a written exam, which she did – answering every question in record time.

'That brings the IQ test to an end now' said the doctor. 'I will of course need time to examine your answers and produce your final result. I've got a feeling yours is going to be something quite exceptional. Now that we've put your brain through its paces I thought it would be all the better for me to let you rest and examine your sleep patterns as we discussed.'

CHAPTER 23

Brooke called Ricki back into the office to join them. She lay down comfortably on the doctor's couch with her head resting on a cushion. Dr Gorman attached a strange device to her. The object looked not completely unlike a badly designed shower cap, similar also to a fishing net, albeit one with small round electrical points or sensors on each of the corners of the wires. These wires were connected to an electrical device next to the couch similar to a heart rate monitor. The device was worn like a wig and covered all of the top part of her head. She looked ridiculous.

Ricki knocked on the door from outside then walked in. Upon sight of Brooke lying on the couch with the device on her head Ricki almost fell to the floor with hysterics.

'What the hell are you wearing!?' she cried out.

Brooke and Dr Gorman both looked at Ricki disapprovingly. Brooke rolled her eyes at her sister. 'I am wearing the sensors for an electroencephalograph machine' she replied.

'An electro...phalo...graph what!?' asked Ricki.

'These machines are highly technical pieces of equipment. They cost thousands of pounds each and they're used to measure your brain wave activity.' added Dr Gorman.

Ricki started reaching into her bag for her phone 'I'm sorry but you just look so stupid. Let me get your picture and I'll put it on Facebook!' she added.

'Don't you dare get your phone out now!' exclaimed Brooke. 'This is serious!'

Ricki took note of her sister's reaction and put her phone back in her bag. Still giggling she came and sat next to Brooke. 'So am I just gonna sit here and watch you sleep again am I!?' she joked.

'Afraid so' replied Brooke.

'I'll shortly be giving you a mild sedative which should put you to sleep for about two to three hours.' said the doctor to Brooke. 'It will unfortunately make you tired for the rest of the day so I don't advise driving or operating heavy machinery afterwards' he added.

'There are five different types of brain waves or electric patterns that each person has. Namely, the Gamma, Beta, Alpha, Theta and Delta Waves. What I am most interested in seeing is your Theta waves. These are brainwaves that occur most often in meditation and sleep. These theta waves are essential for our learning, memory, and intuition. With theta waves our senses are withdrawn from the external world and focused on signals originating from inside our brain. While you're asleep I'll be actively making notes and monitoring your recordings.' said the doctor.

Dr Gorman walked into his stationery cupboard and could be heard opening some kind of cabinet. While he was gone Ricki started whispering to Brooke.

'How did your IQ test go? she asked her.

'Pretty good I think' replied Brooke in all modesty. 'I think I might need to wait a few days for my final results though' she added.

Dr Gorman walked back in holding a syringe in his hand. He approached Brooke and sat down next to her while flicking at the syringe to remove any air bubbles. 'If you could just hold out your arm for me please' he said to Brooke.

Brooke did as he instructed then Dr Gorman took hold of Brooke's arm with his left hand and with his right he held the syringe just above it prepared to inject.

'If you're ready I shall inject you now?' he enquired.

'Yes I'm ready' replied Brooke.

The doctor gently pierced her skin with the needle and slowly injected the sedative into her vein.

The liquid was injected into Brooke's arm and only took a few moments to empty. Brooke gave a small flinch when the needle first went in but afterwards she looked up and smiled at Ricki and the doctor.

'The sedative should only take a matter of seconds to get to work' he said.

After a few seconds the sedative took its hold on Brooke. She closed her eyes before her head fell back gently onto the cushion. She was now already fast asleep. Ricki and Dr Gorman sat watching over Brooke for several minutes while she lied in front of them. The doctor made them both some coffee while they waited for Brooke's sleep to progress.

◆

CHAPTER 24

A short time passed and at first the readings on the recording equipment were relatively normal. The doctor made regular checks and took a few notes at several intervals. He seemed satisfied that nothing was out of the ordinary.

'How did she get on with her IQ test' Ricki asked the doctor. 'She seemed to think she did quite well which for her usually means that she stormed through it effortlessly!' she added.

'Indeed' replied the doctor, pausing before he said his next words. 'Her results were...extraordinary to say the least, so much so that I must ask a colleague of mine for a second opinion.' he added.

'You have no idea!' insisted Ricki. 'She is the cleverest person I've ever known. When she was at school they said she used to show the teachers how to run the class. Her friends called her the teachers' teacher. She got straight As in all her subjects, Maths, English, Science, Business, French, Spanish, Art and more. It's rare that she got less than 100% in all her exams. If she did then they would normally blame the teacher for something they did wrong!'

'That's very interesting' replied the doctor.

A few more minutes passed and Brooke's physical and mental condition began to change. Her breathing became noticeably heavier and her eyes began to blink and move faster. Ricki noted the changes. She recognised them perfectly from when she had watched her sister sleep before.

'What is that that's happening to her eyes?' she asked Dr Gorman.

'It's called Rapid Eye Movement, or R.E.M. for short' replied the doctor 'It's a sign that she's dreaming but she shouldn't be having this for at least another hour into her sleep. She's only been asleep for fifteen minutes yet she's starting to display symptoms that most people wouldn't have until after an hour and a half.'

He glanced over at the monitor and a look of shock fell over his face. 'My lord!!' he said 'Her readings are going crazy!'

The readings on the monitor had very quickly gone from normal with relatively small movement along the axis to the point where they had now shown readings flying from one far side of the screen to the other, and beyond.

'What does that mean?' asked Ricki.

'I'm not really sure' he replied 'What we're seeing

on the screen suggests that she is certainly dreaming but she's having dreams so vivid that it's like she's dreaming within her dream. Her readings are off the chart, I've never seen anything like this!' he added.

Ricki remained silent. She didn't know what to say since she knew more than she was able to let on.

Brooke continued to sleep for about another hour and a half during which time the doctor continued to take readings and make notes at regular intervals. When his tests were finished he switched off his equipment, disconnected Brooke from the electroencephalograph machine and carefully removed the device from her head. She slowly opened her eyes.

'Hi sleepy head!' said Ricki.

Brooke remained silent, still incoherent and unable to respond she faded in and out of her sleep for several minutes. She finally came round from her sleep, sat up on the sofa and drank some water through a straw which the doctor offered her.

'She's unlikely to remember much, or indeed any of this afterwards' said the doctor addressing Ricki. 'I wouldn't advise using public transport. I'll book you a taxi to take you both straight home. I'll need some time to check through my notes and findings so I'll be in contact with her sometime in the next two to three days to confirm her results, and where we go from there.' he added.

The taxi soon arrived and after drinking more water Brooke stumbled to her feet. Weak and partially crippled with fatigue Ricki held her arm to steady her as they walked out the office to the waiting car.

When they arrived home Ricki helped Brooke to her bedroom. She remained silent, too tired to speak. Ricki moved her to the bed, took her shoes off then left the bedroom. Closing the door behind her as her sister slept she strolled into the living room to finally sit down and relax for the first time that day.

CHAPTER 25

Following her busy day Brooke slept right through until morning. Ricki got up around the same time and they passed the day away by watching some films and TV shows that they liked, and doing a few household chores.

When night time came the two of them couldn't wait to get back to Brooke's bedroom and reprise their previous roles, Brooke once again lying in bed with Ricki sitting over her.

'I've got a feeling you're not gonna need me to do this much longer' stated Ricki. 'I think pretty soon you'll be taking control of your dream state all by yourself' she added.

'I hope you're right' replied Brooke. 'Now I'll need you to guide me through advancing my abilities. We've done walking, running and even jumping. Now I want to tear up the rule book completely and try flying. I want to be able to levitate and move through the air'. she added.

'How do we do that then?' asked Ricki.

'Talk to me just like you've done before, then simply tell me to do it' replied Brooke.

Ricki watched over Brooke once again as she lay down and fell asleep. Brooke's breathing became heavier and her eyes began to twitch - Rapid Eye Movement.

In her dream Brooke found herself in the same place she was two nights ago. It was quiet and peaceful, no cars or traffic. No pedestrians. No noise, just trees and plants. She was in the field again. She heard Ricki's voice calling her.

'Brooke' she uttered.

Her sister then appeared in front of her.

'Brooke' she uttered again. 'It's me Ricki'.

Brooke remained calm and in control of her thoughts. She knew where she was and what she needed to do.

'Remember where you are again, you're in a dream state. Keep calm and concentrate. You want to try and start flying. Look around you and see yourself first, see everything else around you.' said Ricki. 'Now imagine yourself levitating slowly off the ground just like we said'.

Brooke wasted no time in responding. She no longer had any fear or doubt in her about what she could do. She looked down at the ground below her feet then began to start pushing herself upwards. Sure enough her feet slowly began to rise above the soil. First she managed to gain a whole inch between the soles of her feet and the ground. She then pushed harder and gained another inch. She gradually pushed herself up and up further and further until she was floating a whole twelve inches from the terrain of the field.

'Now push yourself higher still' said Ricki 'Keep going higher and higher until you're as high as a house, then higher still' she said.

Brooke obeyed her sister's command and gradually levitated higher. The ground became further and further away from her as she gained more and more altitude. She had now reached a new height of more than thirty feet. Not content with achieving this height she pushed herself further and further still. Her movement gained momentum and she became faster and faster as she rised ever more upwards. She began to feel the wind on her face. Her hair and clothing were moving as the air rushed past. She climbed higher and higher still. She was now several hundred feet from the ground.

'Now come back down' said Ricki, who was somehow still understood from a long distance away on the ground.

Brooke responded by falling back to earth, quickly to start with, then slowly as she approached the ground closer, until she came to a very gentle stop and landed softly back on the ground.

'I assume you've now mastered how to levitate up and down?' said Ricki 'Now let's try and moving forwards and heading somewhere. Look ahead of you see those trees in the distance. Now see yourself flying towards one of them'.

With that Brooke slowly began to levitate upwards and floated forwards in the direction of the trees. It was a diagonal movement to start with. She reached the same height as the trees but was still some distance away. She glanced down at the ground from where she was, then glanced forward at the trees. Beaming with happiness at her progress she then inched forward towards the trees at speed. She reached the trees in an instant. Floating alongside one of them she reached out and grabbed a leaf off a top branch. Glancing at it the detail was incredible. Bright green, from the bottom of the stem to the top of the shoot she could make out the minute hairs and fir of the leaf sticking out. The veins and arteries covered the underside in all directions. It wasn't symmetrical but jagged. It was unique yet all its imperfections were perfect. It was just like a real one.

'Once you've done that, you can try flying in all directions' said Ricki from the ground below her looking up.

In response Brooke let go of the leaf. It floated towards the ground slowly. She then turned her attention back to flying. She looked away in the distance at the horizon, and with a deep breath she leapt forward. Still with an upward stance she moved at great speed through the air. Like before she felt the wind more and more as she gathered speed. Her velocity increased further and further at an increasing rate. She decided to try moving up and down. Firstly she flew upwards in a diagonal direction then she came back down again, in a gracious curve, all while moving at speeds faster than an airplane. She had now mastered it. She could go anywhere and do anything in her dreams.

She gradually came to a halt then floated back down to earth gently and stood still on the ground. She was ready to wake up now and share the news of what she had done with Ricki. By simply willing it to happen she bought herself back to reality. She opened up her eyes in bed and shot up from her pillow.

'I did it, I did it!!' she blurted out with excitement. 'I managed to fly. It was amazing!! Even better than running and jumping. I can do anything now'! she added sitting up in bed.

Ricki looked at her smiling. 'I'm glad you did it then. I think my work here is done now.' she said.

CHAPTER 26

A blurry image appeared. It was dark and gloomy. Shadowy with textures and outlines overlapped. The scene was that of housing. Terraces and high rises could be seen in all directions. Parked cars obstructed the footpaths with two wheels on one side to make space for traffic along the carriageway. Pedestrian movement was limited to a narrow space. Vision was impaired by stationery vehicles, more so the large 4x4s and vans. People strolled along the footpath clearly daunted by what they saw on the ground. Something was on the path that people avoided. The object was side-stepped and stepped over. The impediments along the footway made the object difficult to observe from afar.

Brooke emerged in the middle of the street. She was instantaneously aware of her circumstances. Clothed in her night dress she looked down at her hands and feet. For the first time ever she was an interloper in her own dream and not an observer from the outside. She could turn and walk, run and fly. She glanced all around her hoping something might reveal her location. The only clue she observed was a sign across the street that read 'WELDON ROAD'.

She gazed at the people passing by and observed their agitated reaction to the object. What was it? She had to discern for herself so she walked closer. In between two parked cars on the foot-path was a gap covering a distance close to ten feet. In the centre of that gap there was a hole in the ground, a square hole measuring no less than three feet wide. A manhole without the manhole cover. Perhaps the cover was missing or stolen.

Brooke gazed at the cover feeling somewhat con-fused. It's just a drainhole cover that's missing its lid she thought to herself. How can this be any real danger? She began to shift closer to the open-ing expecting to see where the hole was leading. Her confusion had turned to curiosity. As she ap-proached the hole she could view the drop from an angle. Expecting to see the base of the hole she advanced closer, yet the bottom never appeared. Her curiosity now became concern. Just how deep was this hole? From her current angle she could see more than five feet below ground level. Peer-ing down the hole she edged closer still, she could see ten feet below, fifteen feet below and still falling deeper. Within moments her concern had turned to disbelief. Her disbelief turned to shock. Her shock turned to horror.

Standing at the far edge of the opening with her

eyes gazing down the pit she looked and saw the whole cavern that burrowed into the ground below her. The initial drop widened considerably into a cavern-like burrow thirty feet deep. Daylight from above illuminated the base of the hole covered with sharp uneven cracks and small crevices leading in all directions. If anyone fell down there they would certainly not be clambering out.

Hearing footsteps behind her Brooke turned to see pedestrians approaching. The first was an elderly lady with a wheel cart. She squeezed past the side of the car that obscured her vision of the open hole. Moving away from the hole towards the elderly lady Brooke began to panic for that person's safety. She held out her hands out to block the lady's path as she approached closer.

'Look out'! She bellowed. 'There's a hole in the ground in front of you'.

The elderly lady ignored Brooke's endeavour to stop and walked straight through her like a holographic light projection. She was oblivious to her and continued on her course heading straight for the open manhole.

Brooke was initially shocked that the lady had quite literally walked through her with complete indifference, totally unaware that she was even there. She then turned around and continued to holler at the lady.

'Look out!' she insisted. 'Look out! Look where

you're walking!'

Despite Brooke's persistence the lady was un-phased by her attempts to stop her. The lady was now only inches from certain death as she ap-proached the pit and Brooke was about to give up hope of her observing the hole in time to avoid it, when suddenly the lady gazed down in horror and came to a very abrupt halt. She stopped suddenly and peered down into the hole in shock. She stood for a moment at the edge of the opening where Brooke was standing only seconds earlier, then proceeded to walk around the edge of the hole and onwards along the footway.

The next pedestrian approached. A young man smartly dressed in a suit. Reacting comparably to before Brooke turned to face the man and raced towards him. Arms held out she once again strived to physically block his way, ordering him to stop and look. Her endeavour was very much in vain. He walked through her like a ghost and could neither see nor hear her. Brooke grew in-creasingly hysterical. She knew the reason why she was invisible to him yet she still persisted with her efforts. After being walked through again she turned to see the man approach the hole. She persisted with shouting at him to look when all of a sudden the man glanced down in horror, much like the lady before him. Close to gasping with shock and the feeling of the unexpected he quickly came to a stop just at the edge of the hole and continued to gaze down into the pit. Had he seen the lady before do the same or was he just being observant? Either way he was aware of the danger and how to avoid it.

The man carefully walked around the hole, much like the lady before him, then continued his journey along the footpath away from the hazard. Brooke felt an enormous sigh of relief at watching him avoid a potentially fatal accident. Despite being oblivious at her attempt to prevent the terrible calamity all she truly cared about was that the disaster was avoided. Feeling an air of ease Brooke watched the man walk away. Perhaps there was no real danger after all if everyone could see for themselves then they should avoid it, right?

Brooke's awareness was then painfully disrupted. Hearing a noise she quickly turned to see another pedestrian approach. A teenage girl, short and slim with long red hair, whose attention was entirely corrupted by the text message she was scrutinising on her mobile phone. Brooke's unearthly face turned white. A site like this is dangerous at the best of times but on this occasion the consequences would be catastrophic. Brooke once again dashed towards her waving her arms to get the girl's attention.

'STOP!' she shouted. This time even more emphatically than before. The girl remained unresponsive to her command. 'STOP!!' she shouted again even louder than last time.

Oblivious to her own mortal danger the teenage girl continued to march in the same direction with eyes fixated on her phone. Walking right through her like a ghost as the last two people did the endeavour to block her proved futile as the girl was equally oblivious to Brooke. It ultimately dawned on Brooke that there was nothing she could do for her. The accident was inevitable. As she watched the girl approach the hole Brooke was compelled to cover her eyes unable to truly witness the horrifying ordeal.

CHAPTER 27

Brooke's anguish caused so much distress that she awoke in her bed with eyes already flooded with tears. The incident was truly heart breaking for her. She sat up in bed sobbing. What she had witnessed seemed to resonate with her more deeply than ever before. The progress she had made with the interaction of her own entity had come at a cost. She made her experience more intense. The trauma felt more personal and she truly cared for her victim now more than ever. She continued to sob on her own. The door to her bedroom swung open and Ricki strolled in. Brooke's blubbering had woken her up. As Ricki approached the bed she knelt beside her sister while putting her arms out to comfort her. Brooke remained seated in the same position facing forward.

'What's wrong?' asked Ricki.

'I couldn't stop it' replied Brooke.

Without the need to ask any more questions Ricki knew exactly what she meant. Since she struggled to find the right words of comfort she decided it was best to remain silent. The two sisters stayed side by side for the rest of the night until morning, though Brooke hardly slept.

CHAPTER 28

Daylight eventually arrived and Brooke arose from bed as soon as sunlight glared through her curtains. Despite her mournful state of mind she spared a thought for her sister's peaceful slumber in bed next to her. Remaining soundless she crept out her bedroom without unsettling Ricki. She closed the door gently behind her then tip-toed to the kitchen. She prepared herself some coffee and sat down at the table.

She remained silent and pensive throughout. All her thoughts were focussed on the hardship of her ordeal from the previous night. The graphic nature of her experience made her predicament a hard burden to bear. She felt an even bigger weight on her shoulders than she had ever felt. Knowing that she couldn't save the young lady's life in her dream she felt partly responsible for her tragedy.

How was she now going to save all these people? She had achieved so much in her progress with her dream state. Her super human abilities made her like a goddess in her dreams yet she was still unable to do the one thing she had set out to do all along.

The radio and TV were switched off creating an almost eerie silence. She engrossed herself in her thoughts for several hours and waited with restraint until Ricki awoke. Strolling into the kitchen she saw Brooke sitting in silence with her empty coffee cup in hand. The absence of noise in the room generated an increased level of self-consciousness between the two of them.

'You OK?' said Ricki.

'No not really' replied Brooke.

Ricki sympathised with her sister but couldn't think of anything more to say. She poured herself some coffee and sat down next to Brooke.

'Thanks for staying with me last night' said Brooke.

'That's OK, you don't have to thank me' replied Ricki 'You'd do the same for me and more still' she added.

Touching her sister's hand Brooke smiled gently in response.

'I don't know what I'm supposed to do next' she said. 'I watched someone die like I was there with her and I couldn't stop it'. she added

'Is there anything else you saw that might be of use? asked Ricki. 'Did you see when or where it might happen? Was there anything that gave it away that you can remember'?

'No, nothing' replied Brooke while deep in thought. 'It was just a normal street with lots of cars and people walking past. There was nothing that gave it...' she then paused in thought.

Noticing her pause Ricki became very curious. 'What is it?' she asked her.

'Hold on a second' Brooke said with intrigue. 'There was something I remember, a street name on the sign. It read WELDON ROAD.'

'Well that's a start' replied Ricki. 'You never know. If we can find that street then we might just have a chance of stopping it, hold on a second' she added.

Ricki darted out the kitchen back to her bedroom where she grabbed her tablet. Rushing back in to the kitchen she sat back down with Brooke at the table and switched on her device. She began browsing the internet while Brooke observed with great intrigue. 'If we can find the street name you mentioned then maybe we can find the exact place where the accident happened.' she said.

Ricki opened up the search engine page then typed in the words WELDON ROAD.

'Right there's three streets that match that name.' One of them is in Corby, Northamptonshire, another one is in Oxford, and the last is in Highbury, North London.' She explained. 'Do you remember anything about the street? she asked

'I remember a row of terraced houses stretching all along the street.' replied Brooke. They were old fashioned. Victorian style I think, but I only saw a small section of the street, about 50 or 60 yards max' she added.

'That might be all we need to know' replied Ricki. 'If I use the street view then we can look at all of these roads to see if you can recognise them'. she added. 'Let's take a look at the first one in Altrincham' she continued. 'Does that look like the right street to you?' she asked, turning her tablet to Brooke.

Brooke picked up Ricki's tablet and began to study the image closely. She flicked her finger across the screen to view more of the street.

'No' she replied. 'The houses are completely different'. She added, handing her tablet back to Ricki.

Ricki scrolled back to the previous page on her tablet then clicked on another address.

'OK, what about this one in Oxford' she asked her.

Brooke looked again at her tablet examining the street on the screen for a few moments. Nothing that she saw looked at all familiar.

'Nope' she replied.

Ricki once again scrolled back to the previous page on her tablet then clicked on another address.

'OK, what about this one in Highbury?' she asked.

'That's familiar looking' she replied with a certain amount of intrigue. She began to peruse the street through the use of the touch screen function. She analysed everything in detail scrolling along each section, zooming in and out on specific buildings and objects. Her attention turned ever more serious when she came across a site that was all too familiar.

'That's it!' she insisted emphatically. 'That part there' she added pointing at the screen.

'That's the street that was in your dream?' asked Ricki.

'That's what I saw. I recognise it like I was there' replied Brooke.

'So what do we do now then?' asked Ricki. 'Is it possible to find out when the accident is going to occur?' she added.

'I don't know' replied Brooke 'I had no way of seeing what the time was' she added.

Gazing down at the kitchen floor with her palms to her forehead Brooke buried herself in her thoughts. She pondered rigorously hard for several moments. Eager for her sister to reveal Ricki then intervened.

'Is there anything you can think of that can help

you to determine the time of day?' she asked

'Yes!' replied Brooke, glancing back up at her from the floor. 'I remember seeing the shadows of the cars and objects along the street.'

Bewildered, Ricki gazed back at her with a mystified demeanour.

'How does that help you with determining the time'!? She exclaimed.

'Shadows are created when an object, like a building, blocks out light from the sun. The length of the shadow depends on how low or high the Sun is in the sky' replied Brooke in a patronising tone of voice.

'Yes I know that thanks!' replied Ricki.

'Well' said Brooke. She then continued 'We know that the sun rises in the east and sets in the west and using the map we can already determine the exact GPS of the location. I remember that one of the cars parked along the east side of the street near to the accident was a Volkswagen Type 2 Camper van'.

Deep in thought as she was speaking Brooke stood up from her chair and began pacing up and down the kitchen floor.

'The height of a Camper van is about two metres tall and the street where the accident occurred faces roughly from north to south. The width of the road from kerb-to-kerb is about five metres but as far as I could make out the shadow cast by the camper van only covered a small part of the road from where it was parked by the kerb. Now we know that shadows are longer in the beginning and end of the day as the sun passes over from east to west. Therefore the angle and length of the shadow from the Camper van would indicate that the accident occurred shortly before the middle of the day. Now without the proper equipment available to me and just using basic figures off the top of my head I calculate the time to be around 11.30 AM.' she added.

'That's a pretty accurate guess if you ask me!' insisted Ricki.

'Well I also estimate that my calculation falls within a plus or minus 20-30 minute window of error which basically means it could happen any time between 11.00AM and 12.00PM midday. The time now is coming up to 9.00AM which gives us about two or three hours to get there and stop it' added Brooke.

'It shouldn't take more than an hour or so by tube' said Ricki.

'Let's get moving then shall we?' replied Brooke.

Without another minute wasted the sisters both dressed themselves and headed out. They dashed to their nearest tube station to catch the next available train. So far so good.

CHAPTER 29

Luckily the time was after 9.00AM and the station was relatively quiet. Had it been one hour earlier they would not have been so fortunate. The sisters ran through the station forecourt to the barriers scanning their passes. Maintaining a significant lead over Brooke one of the few things she could do better than her older sister was run faster. She dashed down the escalators and along the tunnel on to the platform ahead of her sister. The train had yet to arrive but was due in less than a minute. The short wait for the train's arrival gave Brooke enough time to catch up with her little sister and arrive on the platform.

After pulling in to the station the train doors opened and Ricki hopped on first followed by Brooke who stepped on with less haste. Ricki sat down at the first available seat with Brooke close behind. Sitting down on the tube train next to her sister Brooke examined her watch. The time read 09.14. She knew it took on average 47 minutes journey time to get to her station within plus or minus six minutes - when the trains ran a good service.

Leaning towards Brooke Ricki began to talk. 'So tell me about this girl who has the accident, what does she look like?' she asked her.

'About 5'2", slim build and freckly with long ginger hair, wearing a blue t-shirt and black leggings' said Brooke.

'Should be pretty easy to find with that description' replied Ricki. Brooke nodded.

The train reached its next stop along the line with no hold-ups and more people walked on after others stepped off. The train stood still for several seconds. Just enough time to allow everyone on and off, and to allow time for those who are unsure whether to board the train or not to make up their minds. Expecting the train doors to close and the train to pull away any moment the sisters sat there patiently.

One minute passed and the sisters both slowly started to become a little bit anxious. The train should have left by now so why wasn't it moving? Another minute passed and a familiar crackling sound could be heard coming from the speakers above their heads. It sounded like someone was going to make an announcement. The crackling noise quickly died down and a voice could be heard talking through the train.

'Ladies and gentleman this is the driver speaking, we

apologize for the delay on the train but this is due to a fault on the train in front of us which is holding us up. I'm afraid we cannot move until the fault on the train in front has been fixed so I'm afraid we are gonna have to wait here for the time being. I will keep you up to date as soon as I hear anything more'.

The sisters looked at each other with a slight sense of dread.

'Shit!' exclaimed Ricki. 'What do we do now?' she asked Brooke.

After the initial reaction to the announcement Brooke calmed herself down.

'For now we just wait it out' she replied. 'By my calculation we still have at least one hour and forty minutes to get there so there's no reason to panic, I reckon the train will be on the move again soon. I say we just sit it out here and wait for the train to get moving again' she added.

'OK fine. So long as the train gets moving again soon' said Ricki. 'What if I ran all the way there as fast as I could, do you think I could make it in time?' she asked.

'No there's no way you could run fast all the way there, and even if you could you wouldn't know the way on foot. You'd most likely get lost. Besides which it's too dangerous. You'd probably end up getting killed yourself' said Brooke.

'What are the alternatives?' asked Ricki. 'I mean

we could get a taxi but then we'd have to wait for it to arrive and it would probably get stuck in traffic, and a bus would be even slower.' she added.

'That's right. I'm playing the odds and at the moment this is still the quickest means of travel' insisted Brooke.

'Let's just hope this train gets moving soon then shall we!?' replied Ricki.

CHAPTER 30

Minutes passed by with no more announcements from the train driver, much less the train showing any sign of moving soon, and the sisters were becoming increasingly agitated. Time was running out and both of them knew that if the train didn't leave before long they might not arrive where they needed to in time.

Brooke knew the transport layout of the city and almost all connections. She knew that if they left the tube station to find alternative means of transportation now and traffic was normal for this time of day they could catch a bus which was scheduled to take approximately one hour and 17 minutes within plus or minus nine minutes. Similarly they could travel by taxi which would take approximately 55 minutes within plus or minus five minutes, but the time it would take to book or find one available added an average time of four minutes. Cycling was one alternative but neither she nor Ricki had a bicycle. She would have to buy one from the shop nearby – four minutes away, then she would need to make sure the bike was immediately usable. The process would take an average time of fifteen minutes. To ride a bike to where she needed to get to would take around 40 minutes, 35 if she ignored red lights and traffic laws. Ricki, being faster could in theory make the journey in around 30 minutes but would most likely get lost, not to mention placing both their lives at considerable risk. Running there would take Brooke approximately 52 minutes, and Ricki 44 minutes – if she knew the way and did NOT get lost.

In short she concluded that all viable alternative means of travel and transportation would take approximately one hour or more from their current location so their best option for now was still to wait for the train to move.

The clock was ticking and time was continuing to run out. Brooke once again observed her watch. The time read 09.37. They had only been waiting for 15 minutes but the circumstances made it feel like much, much more.

Shaking her head with doubt and worry Ricki turned to Brooke.

'If this train doesn't get moving soon we're gonna have to find another way of getting there!' she insisted.

'Yes but this is still the fastest way' said Brooke. 'I've done the calculations in my head of all different options available' she added.

'So what's your conclusion then?' asked Ricki.

'In a nutshell this train needs to move within the next 20 minutes without further interruptions for us to make it there on time. What's more if we decide to take alternative transport we need to do it within roughly the next 15 minutes otherwise the chances of us arriving on time are slim.' replied Brooke.

'Firstly how do you calculate this so accurately!?' asked Ricki 'Also are you saying that if we wait more than 15 minutes we're not likely to get there in time' she added.

'I'm saying that if we wait more than 15 minutes the chances of us arriving on time are greatly reduced' replied Brooke. 'We have to make the choice within the next few minutes – should we wait here and hope that the train moves or find another way of getting there' she added.

'Let's pray we don't have to make that choice' said Ricki.

Several more minutes passed and the sisters sat on the train with increasing unease. Both were worried that soon they'd have to make a difficult decision – should they stay or should they go?

Brooke gazed at her watch regularly. Every second that passed felt like a minute, every minute felt like an hour. Was this train ever going to move and if so, when? There was still no word from the driver and the train had not moved another inch. If they did make the decision to walk off then which mode of travel should they take? Each way had its own advantages as well as its own drawbacks. The noise from other passengers grew lighter as they each in turn became more and more impatient and walked off the train. The train became increasingly quiet until all other passengers walked off and the two of them were the only people left on the carriage.

With a serious gaze Brooke turned to Ricki. 'We have to make the decision now' she said to her. 'We can't wait much longer' she added.

'I can't make that decision!' replied Ricki dismissively. 'We're both here because of you so you have to make the decision'.

'OK we can't risk it any longer, let's go' replied Brooke insistently.

The two of them stood up from their seats and made their way to the doors of the train to step off. At that point a familiar noise began to resound through the train. A clamour of crackling echoed around the carriage. It was the loudspeaker. Could it be that the train driver was about to make an announcement? The crackling noise continued for a few seconds then the line became clearer. The driver was indeed about to make an announcement. The girls stopped in their tracks and listened with complete and undivided attention.

'Good morning again ladies and gentlemen this is the driver speaking. I apologize for the delay in updating you with the current situation but I am happy to inform you that the problem on the train in front has now been resolved and the train will soon be on the move, once again I apologize for the delay and for any inconvenience this may have caused'

Breathing a huge sigh of relief the two sisters sat back down at their seats. This had to be the happiest any loudspeaker announcement had ever made them. They had never been so joyed to hear a message over a radio. The two of them still had some chance of making it to their destination on time. They glanced at each other grinning with delight.

The rest of the sisters' journey on the tube was quite agreeable. The train moved relatively quickly between stations without any more hold ups.

CHAPTER 31

The ladies arrived at their planned station of choice. The longest distance had now been covered but they had to do the rest of the journey on foot. They knew the street name and how to get there. Brooke looked at her watch once more. The time read 10.39AM. She knew the street was roughly 20 minutes away by walking distance, or ten minutes if they ran. Brooke already had the optimum route planned out in her head. She had memorized the map to her destination in its entirety and she was now feeling confident of achieving what she had set out to do, confident of saving that young ladies' life.

Walking out of the tube station entrance the two of them turned left immediately and following Brooke's directions proceeded north along the street at a swift pace, just short of running speed. All seemed well with the progress of their journey when something of concern began to reveal itself.

Advancing closer and closer to the end of the street the two of them remained silently fixed on a sight which stole their attention from each other. It was difficult to make out from a great distance due to the presence of other pedestrians, cars and trees obscuring their view, but as they drew nearer and nearer it quickly became apparent.

At the north end of the street was a four way junction. What they came across was a construction site which spread from one side of the street to the other. The street had been completely blocked off at the north end by temporary wooden fencing put up by construction workers to stop trespassers. The sturdy fence panels were ten feet tall and covered the entire width of the street with no visible way of getting through. Neither Brooke nor Ricki had the agility to climb over these panels, nor could they see any possible entrance through it that was open or unlocked.

They approached the construction site in disbelief. Demoralized once again by this unfortunate turn of events they looked at each other completely disheartened.

'Shit!' cried Ricki. 'What the hell are we gonna do now!? she added.

'I don't know' replied Brooke. 'We can't go through it by the looks of it and we certainly can't go over it. We'll just have to run back' she added.

The two of them wasted no time. They immediately turned around and made off in the opposite direction, back the way they came albeit at an even faster walk than before. Ricki, being the fastest sped off in front of her sister and Brooke was forced to start a running pace to keep up with her. The street, since it was blocked at the far end was largely free of traffic and oncoming vehicles so Brooke decided to run down the middle of the road to speed up further, avoiding obstacles and other pedestrians along the footpath. Ricki caught sight of her sister who had managed to gain a lead on her and decided to follow suit. Time was running out and before long the sisters were racing down the central stretch of road together. Ricki once again gained the upper hand on Brooke, proving she could yet again outpace her sister.

They ran the whole length of the street back the way they came, past the station they had exited a few minutes earlier to the junction at the far end. They took a sharp left turn and headed east towards a busy main road. They reached the next junction where they were met by a daunting spectacle.

The street was a bustling retail area. Department stores, fashion outlets, restaurants, banks and supermarkets lined the back length of the streets on both sides. To make matters worse it was market day. Opposite them along the kerbline of the footpaths were market stools of every sort. Street vendors were selling clothes, toys, beauty products, souvenirs and more. Hordes of pedestrians and buyers swarmed the length and breadth of the street as far as they both could see. People were moving in all directions, in and out of shops and stalls, intertwining in each other's individual routes. Despite the high concentration of footfalls there was still a steady stream of traffic moving along the road in each direction. This was a traditional street market - an increasingly rare sight in modern day London.

The sisters both let out a shriek of horror and despair.

'Oh my god, tell me this isn't happening!' declared Ricki.

How could this come about to them now? Wrestling their way through this mass crowd would be a time consuming trial in itself without the need for them to proceed.

'We don't have time for this' insisted Brooke. 'We have to move fast. Come with me' she added while grabbing Ricki by the hand and leading her straight into the middle of the road in front of a moving car.

The driver slammed on the brakes and the car shrieked to a halt. Missing them both by inches the vehicle stopped right beside them. The driver leaned out of his window to shout angry abuse at them both.

'What the hell are you doing!? he bellowed.

Ricki flinched in terror and closed her eyes

while Brooke remained focused and relatively un-phased. She ignored the driver's obscenities and continued to drag Ricki with her along the stretch of carriageway.

'What are you doing!?' demanded Ricki. 'You're going to get us both killed' she added.

'Trust me' insisted Brooke. 'This is the only way we can get through this crowd in time.' she added.

'What by running down a busy main road in front of all the cars!' exclaimed Ricki.

'It's the only way, trust me' insisted Brooke. 'We are definitely not gonna die here! I promise you.'

As they ran along the street through the middle of the road the car that almost hit the two sisters had now started moving, slower than usual due to being stuck behind the two of them. The driver leaned out of his window yet again and proceeded to scream at them further.

'GET OUT OF THE WAY!' he yelled continuously.

Brooke remained undeterred by the driver and persisted to scurry along the stretch of main road. The crowd along the street had now become very aware of what they were doing. Heads had turned and all eyes were on them as they dashed past with traffic moving slowly behind them. They ran for several hundred yards past the main section of the retail area until the crowds of pedestrians eventually dwindled.

With her sisters hand still gripped tightly in hers Brooke observed the space now available along the footpath and headed off the road and onto the pavement.

'You can let go of me now!' insisted Ricki as they ran along the street.

Brooke acknowledged her sister and released her grip on Ricki's hand. The cars behind them resumed their original speed, carried on and sped past them. Brooke and Ricki continued along the footpath for a short distance then made a left turn into a side street off the main road. The journey was far from over. They still had several streets to make it past and time was potentially now very limited.

'Which way is it from here' enquired Ricki as the two of them ran side-by-side along the street.

'To the end of this road, then we turn right, then we take the second turning on the left' replied Brooke now panting as she struggled to simultaneously speak while running.

They continued on with their journey on foot until they encountered a sight that was eerily familiar to them. This street was what they had looked at on the tablet earlier today.

In front of them they saw the same railway bridge that led to the street they were heading for. The bridge stood high above the railway line constructed of a long steep ramp on each side. There were no stairs. Something captured Brooke's attention. It was the young lady she saw in her dream near the bottom of the ramp on the opposite side. Though she was not distracted by her mobile phone in her hand at this point the girl was instantly recognizable to Brooke. Her clothing alone made her stick out from a mile away, not to mention her striking red hair.

The two of them noticed that a train was quickly approaching. Not just any train either – a large freight train with dozens of carriages. This could not have happened at a more inconvenient time.

'That's her', exclaimed Brooke 'That's the girl I saw in my dream'.

'HEY YOU!' they shouted at the top of their voices.

Their attempts at grasping the girl's attention proved fruitless. The thunderous roar of the approaching train drowned out their shouting as well as all other noises nearby.

'It's no use' shouted Brooke 'There's no way she's gonna hear us with the noise of this train passing us. We have to get over this bridge and catch her'.

With the realization that they could not be heard they dashed for the ramp leading up over the railway. Brooke now knew that they only had a matter of seconds, not minutes to act. Still calling out to the girl they sprinted to the top of the ramp where it reached the overpass. Oblivious to what was going on behind her on the bridge the girl by now had crossed the railway line and casually strolled forward onto the street in her intended direction towards the spot of her impending death. Feeling a faint vibration from her pocket she took out her mobile phone and gazed at the screen.

The two sisters crossed the overpass to the opposite side. Running ahead of her sister Ricki reached the opposite side of the overpass first then raced down the ramp towards the bottom. Still drowned out by the ear-splitting noise from the freight train she carried on crying out to the girl, in vain. Brooke followed closely behind her.

After reaching the bottom of the ramp Ricki darted along the street, the girl now less than a hundred yards from her. With her attention focused solely on the girl in the distance a large stone lay on the pavement directly in Ricki's path, completely obscured by her tunnel vision. Without any awareness of the stone's existence Ricki stepped on it with the centre of her foot causing her ankle to twist forward and to the side against her will. This forceful manoeuvre in the change of her dynamic body movement at great speed forced her to completely lose her balance and tumble to the floor.

Brooke witnessed her sister plummet to the ground. Catching up to her in an instant she had the instinct to come to her aid and slowed down to an almost complete stop nearly forgetting the bigger issue at hand.

'Are you alright?' she asked her. Lying face down on the ground Ricki looked up. Unable to move at this time from the pain and shock of her ordeal she pointed frantically at the girl down the road.

The only sound she could utter was the word 'Go!' in a very broken and desperate voice.

Brooke acknowledged her sister's instruction and carried on running down the street towards the girl. Realizing that her shouting was getting no-where she simply had to bolt as fast as she could down the street to catch the girl before it was too late. She ran faster than she had ever run in her life and was gaining ground on the girl.

Still oblivious to all that was going on the girl con-tinued to stroll along the pavement completely engrossed in what was happening on her phone. She approached nearer and nearer to the infernal hole where Brooke had seen the tragedy in her dream. Her feet were one footstep away from falling when all of a sudden two arms were flung around the waist of her body. Within an instant she felt herself being thrown to the side and into the road. The force was such that the girl had no time whatsoever to react and fell on to the ground in the middle of the road. It was Brooke.

Pointing at the hole Brooke stood over her on the

kerb line trying to explain what was going on.

'Sorry' she said while panting with exhaustion. 'Big hole there…' she blurted out.

Clearly mortified at these sudden events the girl looked at Brooke in horror. Still lying on the ground she then looked at where Brooke was pointing and began to understand the essence of what had just happened.

Apologizing emphatically Brooke helped her on to her feet and tried to explain why she had done what she did to her. It was technically an assault despite her having no other choice to save her life.

After taking some time to reflect on events the girl reluctantly thanked Brooke for what she did and began to stroll off without serious injury, still in a mental state of shock and confusion.

'Just remember to be careful where you're walking' Brooke cried out.

Turning round the girl nodded her head in acknowledgement then continued on her way.

Brooke's attention was now turned to Ricki. She had just remembered that her sister had fallen over and could be badly injured. Turning around she saw that Ricki had now managed to scramble to her feet. Bruised and battered, with a twisted ankle Ricki started to limp towards her.

'Are you alright?' asked Brooke.

'I'll be OK' said Ricki.

Moving closer to each other the two sisters began to laugh with relief at what had happened. This was a ground breaking occasion. They had saved their first person.

'We did it. We saved her' boasted Brooke. 'YOU did it. YOU saved her!' insisted Ricki.

Physically and mentally exhausted the two of them inched closer still to each other until they were within reach. With tears of joy they hugged in celebration.

CHAPTER 32

The two sisters had turned their space along the pavement into a kind of resting place. Indifferent to the confused attention of pedestrians and cars passing by they both laid down side-by-side in full stretch with their backs to the ground. Facing up to the sky Brooke reached into her bag, took out her mobile phone and began to dial a number, each press of the keypad giving off a lite electrical tone. Shifting her head slowly towards her Ricki was curious.

'Who are you calling?' she asked

'The local council' replied Brooke. 'I want to report a potentially dangerous hazard on their streets!' she added.

'Good idea' replied Ricki, facing back up at the sky.

Her figure remained still. While gazing at the clouds Brooke was eventually put through to the correct department to whom she reported the hazard. She ended the call then returned the mobile phone to her bag.

Without a sound the two sisters lay motionless for several minutes. Neither of them uttered a word. With their hearts beating slower their adrenaline levels returned to normal. Their work here was done. They were content to recharge their minds and bodies. All of a sudden Ricki broke the long silence with a line profoundly befitting of her.

'Fancy a drink?' she asked

A slight pause ensued. Brooke remained in what was now a carefree state of mind. Slow to produce any response she lethargically turned to Ricki.

'Yeah OK then' she replied silently.

The two of them sluggishly climbed to their feet and headed back the way they came. With Ricki limping on her twisted ankle they walked back over the railway bridge towards the main road near to the market where they had held up traffic earlier. Sighting a pub on a corner close by they agreed to go inside.

CHAPTER 33

Outside the entrance of the pub stood a petite middle-aged lady smoking a cigarette by herself. There were two picnic tables with beer mats on for customers to sit alfresco when the weather was nice. They walked past the elderly lady and entered the pub through the door on the corner. The pub was an old fashioned but well-kept, cozy establishment. The floors were topped with a dark red carpet and the walls were varnished in a rustic brown. Photographs of local celebrities hung in full view and a large mirror behind the well-stocked bar attempted to amplify the undersized scale of the public house.

Guzzling his pint and munching his crisps the only other customer in the house was an elderly overweight man sitting at the bar. Clearly a regular here the man gazed at the two young ladies in surprise. He was not used to having sight of two young women in his pub so early. This was not their usual establishment after all.

Ignoring that they felt somewhat out of place the girls approached the bar where they were met by a small middle-aged man with grey receding hair.

'Hello there' he said in a friendly welcoming voice. 'What can I get you?' he added.

Brooke stood at the bar first.

'Two large whiskeys with ice please' she blurted out.

Ricki then nodded at Brooke and the barman in agreement then turned around for somewhere to sit. They both wanted to perch somewhere they could discuss the mornings events strictly in private. Looking around the room and at the man sitting at the bar Ricki was unhappy with her options. Had the little pub been busier the noise and clamour of several other conversations concurrently might have drowned out their own but since they would be the only customers in discussion the men in the bar would have almost certainly been eaves dropping.

'Shall we sit outside?' she asked Brooke. 'OK' she replied without giving it much thought.

Ricki headed back outside and sat down at the table farthest from the door, her ankle still in pain. Brooke paid the barman then with drinks in hand followed on soon after.

'Thanks' said Ricki as Brooke placed the two glasses on the table. The lady who stood outside smoking soon finished her cigarette, stubbed out the end on top of a bin nearby then walked back into the pub. With no-one else in sight this left Brooke and Ricki able to converse without fear of being overheard.

'Do you wanna get that ankle looked at?' asked Brooke. 'No, I'll be fine' insisted Ricki.

'What we did today was a wonderful thing but look at the trouble we went through to get it done' said Brooke. With Ricki nodding in agreement Brooke continued. 'If we're gonna do this we're going to need a much better plan of action in place,' she added.

'Well yes we did have to travel half way across London by tube then run the rest of the way on foot only to have our route blocked by a wall and a busy market, then be almost run over by a convoy of angry drivers, then trip over a stone and fall over! said Ricki. 'Am I supposed to expect this much trouble every time we try to save someone in future?' she added rhetorically.

'That's why we need a proper plan' insisted Brooke. 'We're going to need an organized timetable. I need to be more focussed in my dreams about finding more information. I need to find clues about exact places and times that these accidents are going to happen, street signs, land marks, buildings, anything that gives a clue about the time of day. We have to record it. We can't have a repeat of what happened today.' she added.

'We need to be able to get to these places much

faster' insisted Ricki. 'That means we're gonna need transportation, maps, GPS and sat nav and all that sort of stuff' she added.

'In short, we're gonna need money' insisted Brooke. 'I think we're gonna need to assemble a team as well. We can't do all this by ourselves' she added.

'What like in those crime caper movies where the main character has to put together an elite team of expert safe crackers and computer nerds to break into a bank and steal the money and jewels!?' joked Ricki.

'Something like that, except I don't intend to rob a bank or steal any money!' she added. 'What we need to do is devise a very quick money making scheme.'

'What, like betting on a horse!?' joked Ricki.

Brooke's face lit up. Reflecting deeply on what Ricki said she paused for a brief moment then pointed at her in contentment.

'Yes that's not a bad idea!' she told her. 'All we need to do is find a horse with the most ludicrous odds of winning that's going to race sometime soon, make a bet on it then take our money and run' she added.

'Just like that eh!?' laughed Ricki. 'You're just gonna find a three-legged blind horse with odds of like 500:1 then bet all your savings in the hope of it making you rich!? she added.

'You're along the right lines but I don't intend to do just any old bet' replied Brooke. 'I want to keep a look out for the perfect moment to make a gamble. It's just a case of being in the right place at the right time.' she insisted.

'You don't know anything about horse racing though' argued Ricki

'I know a bit, plus I can study it some more. Lots of people earn a living from it' replied Brooke

'So you're gonna become a professional bookie now are ya!? joked Ricki.

'In a manner of speaking' replied Brooke.

CHAPTER 34

For a day in January the weather was relatively mild and the temperature soared as the sun rose in the sky while the two sisters continued their conversation outside the pub. They had promptly finished their drinks after which Brooke stood up to her feet.

'Fancy another one?' she asked Ricki.

'Yes that will be splendid!' replied Ricki. 'Pint of beer please' she added.

Leaving Ricki outside alone to watch the endless flow of traffic and pedestrians pass by Brooke marched back inside the pub to buy another round.

Drinks in hand, Brooke re-appeared before long. Returning to the table with Ricki she placed both glasses down and sat back in her place.

'Thanks' replied Ricki holding up her glass to take a sip.

Relishing the relaxing heat of the sun together with the soothing flavour of alcohol the two of them remained quiet for a few short moments while they reflected on what was on the forefront of both their minds. Brooke was thinking hard about her plans of making money while Ricki pondered on how all this situation had come about. She broke the silence.

'How do you think you're able to do this then, to see these things happening before they do?' she asked. 'Do you think it's some kind of magical or super natural force that's calling out to you?'

'I don't know' replied Brooke. 'I remember reading a story about ancient tribal shamans that used to believe that the gods would only ever wish for people to die of natural causes, like illness or old age. The gods had control over almost all events and in return for their worship and allegiance they would always be watching over the people so no-one would suffer unnecessarily, but every now and then someone would slip through their grasp.'

Ricki listened with intrigue as Brooke continued.

'They said that when someone would fall victim to a nasty accident the circumstances surrounding the accident would somehow be out of the god's control, so they devised a way of communicating to the people with the intention of saving their lives. Murders were one thing they couldn't stop since they were caused by the evil intention in someone's heart which they couldn't change in itself. But they granted a select few mortal people with psychic abilities in order for them to be able to foresee any accidents with those unlucky people as a way of assisting the gods with their work – the protectors. The legend said the gods would whisper in their ears as they slept, giving them vivid images of what was to become. The gods wanted to protect people from dying without cause' added Brooke.

'Like angels sent down from heaven. Is that what you think you are?' replied Ricki.

'What, an angel with wings and a halo!?' joked Brooke. 'I can't even run that fast let alone fly!' she added.

'Do you believe that's true for you though? Do you believe that you've been gifted with psychic abilities by gods?' asked Ricki.

'I don't know' insisted Brooke. 'What I do know is that there are some people I can save and some I can't. I can't save someone from dying of lung cancer after a lifetime of smoking like that woman who was standing out here, or stop someone from having a heart attack after years of drink and junk food like that man at the bar inside. All I can do is save people from being in the wrong place at the wrong time' she added.

'You're more like a guardian angel then' replied Ricki. 'Maybe the gods have sent you down as a way of helping to correct their wrong doing. You've been putting wrongs right for everyone you know your whole life, now they're just letting you take it even further' she added.

'There could also be a scientific explanation for it too' insisted Brooke.

'What's that then?' asked Ricki.

'I don't know' replied Brooke. 'But I'm sure I can come up with something. For now I'm liking this idea you had about betting on a horse. I'll need to do some more research into this. I've still got my membership to the British library, we can stop there on our way back.' she added.

CHAPTER 35

The two of them finished their second drinks and decided to leave the pub. They headed back down the street to the station where they had arrived earlier. Sitting on the train together Ricki turned her attention to Brooke. Leaning towards and speaking quietly.

'Well done for getting the time of the accident right' she told her. 'It happened between eleven and twelve just like you predicted.' she added.

Brooke then came to a sudden realization. She turned to Ricki to answer. 'Exactly what time do you make it on your watch?' she asked her.

'Right now I make it 12.04PM' replied Ricki.

'Me too' replied Brooke. 'How long were we at the pub for, about 30 minutes would you say'?

'I guess so' replied Ricki. 'Why do you ask?' she added.

Without replying Brooke carried on mumbling and pondering to herself. 'We sat at the pub for about 30 minutes then before that we took about five minutes to walk from where we were lying down. How long would you say we were we lying down for after we saved the girl, about ten minutes?' she said rhetorically. 'That means the accident happened right around....Oh my god!' she said agasp.

Ricki observed the look on Brooke's face. 'What is it?' she asked.

'If my timing's correct that means the accident occurred....would have occurred right around....eleven minutes past eleven.' said Brooke.

'So what?' replied Ricki with cautious indifference. 'That's 11.11' replied Brooke. 'The eleventh minute of the eleventh hour. Don't you know the significance of the number eleven? It's said to have great prophetic and spiritual meaning according to many psychics and astrologers.' she added.

Ricki didn't know how to react. She raised her eyebrows in shock then came to her senses and thought to herself for a moment.

'Do you think that's really true, that it's really got anything to do with it?' she asked her.

'I don't know yet' replied Brooke 'But it is creepy don't you think?'

The train soon reached its destination and both the sisters stepped off. They exited the station and made a brisk walk to the British Library.

When they arrived Brooke wasted no time in finding and retrieving a number of books that she believed to be of use – eight in total, most of which were heavy hardbacks several inches thick and all were renowned reading materials on different aspects of horse racing and the art of skilled gambling.

She packed the books into two rucksacks that she bought nearby, one carried by her, the other by Ricki, then they both headed home.

CHAPTER 36

Upon arriving home Brooke marched straight to the living room with all the books she had borrowed and piled them on the coffee table in the middle. Ricki decided to make some coffee for them both while Brooke began to peruse her books, starting with the biggest.

Ricki walked in to speak to Brooke.

'Want some coffee?' she asked.

Brooke was so engrossed in her book already that her sister's question was unheard. Ricki responded by placing her hand on Brooke's shoulder then giving her a gentle shake.

'Brooke, do you want some coffee? It might be useful' she asked.

'Yeah please' replied Brooke quite abruptly without even lifting her eyes from her book.

Ricki returned to the kitchen and came back soon after with coffee for her and Brooke. She offered one cup to Brooke with the need of placing the drink directly in her line of sight for her to notice.

'Thanks' she replied before taking a few sips, placing the cup down on the table and turning her attention straight back to her book.

Allowing her sister plenty of space Ricki sat down in the armchair. She switched on the TV and turned the sound down low. Without even looking up from her book Brooke was virtually oblivious to her sister and continued to read on with undivided attention.

As Ricki sat and watched her sister scan through the books the speed at which she flew through them left her astounded. Absorbing all the text Brooke finished each page in a matter of seconds. In a matter of minutes she had completely read through the whole publication. She put the book down on one side of the table then picked up another from the pile. She opened the book then began to study it from the first page, all without uttering a word.

Less than one hour passed and Brooke had shot through the whole pile of books on the table. She turned to Ricki who looked at her in awe of what she had just done.

'I finished' she announced.

'So I see!' replied Ricki sarcastically. 'I've sat here and watched in sheer amazement at how fast you've gone through all them books. Were you actually reading through them properly?' she asked.

'Yes they were very insightful. I've learned a hell of a lot but there's still more that I need to research further' replied Brooke. 'I'm gonna read up as much as I can on the internet.' she added.

Brooke left the room and returned shortly after with her laptop. She moved the books to the floor and placed the laptop on the coffee table then and switched it on.

'Do you want some more coffee?' she asked Ricki.

'Yeah please' Ricki replied as she stayed seated in the armchair.

Brooke took the two coffee cups, walked to the kitchen and began making coffee while her laptop was booting up. She walked back in again shortly after with two cups full of coffee. She handed one to Ricki, took a sip of her own then sat down with the laptop on her legs. She spent the next few hours scrutinizing all different websites relating to horse racing and the science behind it, trying to expand her knowledge as much as possible. By now she had already become very enlightened about the industry. The information she learned covered the pedigree of horses, their individual strengths and weaknesses, information about the trainers and jockeys, their roles and competencies, the grounds where they ran, how to study patterns in their wins and losses, injuries, jumping abilities, the weather and so much more.

The whole industry surrounding the sport had become a science to her that she had mastered. Now it was time to put this science into practice.

CHAPTER 37

Seated in the living room the two sisters were exhausted after a long day yet the time was still somewhat early to go to bed. Bored they decided to put a film on. The DVD player started up and the film was about to start. The film was Minority Report, one of Ricki's favourites. She decided to walk off to the bathroom before the film began. With the start of the film being integral to the whole experience she came back in to find that Brooke had not hit the pause button and continued to view the movie resulting in her missing the first few minutes.

'Hey rewind that will ya, I missed the start' she said to Brooke.

'What does it matter!?' she replied.

Ricki looking somewhat annoyed faced her sister. 'You know I like the beginning bit, can't you just rewind it to the exact moment where it starts, all you gotta do is push that rewind button and let it go back' she added.

Brooke's faced turned to a look of excitement. Her

sister's whining had given her a very sudden real-ization.

'Say that again' she said to Ricki.

'I said push that rewind button and take it back to the exact moment where it starts' Ricki insisted.

Pointing her finger in acknowledgement at Ricki, Brooke stood up.

'You've just given me a huge revelation!' she said. Ricki's eyes gazed back at her. She was curious at what her sister was thinking.

'What is it?' she asked Brooke, now with much intrigue.

'After all this time I should have realised!' she said.

'Realised what?' asked Ricki.

'I can't believe I didn't figure this out' added Brooke.

'Figure what out!? asked Ricki.

'It was so obvious' said Brooke.

'What was obvious!!?' exclaimed Ricki, now be-coming increasingly impatient.

'You've made me realise that I can do this in my dream' replied Brooke, DVD remote in hand.

'Do what?' asked Ricki.

'I can control my dreams the same as I can control a film' she replied with great excitement. 'While

I'm in my dreams I can do just about anything, walk, run, even fly. There's no reason why I can't also rewind, fast forward or even pause any of my dreams while I'm in them too. Being in my dreams is just like watching a film on DVD. I can't change any of the events of the film or give it a different ending the same as I wasn't able to change the unfortunate outcome of my dreams but what I can do is view whichever part of the film I want at the push of a button. Similarly I can view any part of my dream I want at will. With these abilities I can control and manipulate time in my dreams as I please. I can even stop time passing completely if I want to while I search around for more clues. I won't need to desperately glance at street signs or clues about locations. I won't need to try and guess the time of day or even the identity of the victim as I'll have the time I need to figure it all out. Wow this is exciting!' she added.

'You really think you can do that?' asked Ricki.

'I know I can' replied Brooke. 'We can work out a detailed plan of it all I'm certain. We can plan the travel and logistics around times of the accidents, locations, victim's descriptions, everything we need to know.'

'You know we're gonna need transport, communication equipment, possibly even some kind of office or HQ' insisted Ricki. 'But before we get all this stuff we're gonna need one thing more than anything – money' she added.

'Leave that to me' replied Brooke.

CHAPTER 38

The two sisters watched the film together in its entirety including the start which Ricki had previously missed. By the time the film had finished the two sisters were feeling tired and decided to call it in for the night.

Brooke went to bed alone and soon fell fast asleep. A blurry image appeared. It was dark and gloomy. Shadowy with textures and outlines overlapping. Brooke found herself once again in her dreams. Standing in her nightgown once again she appeared in the same predicament as usual – unsure of where exactly she was. She could ascertain the distant sound of car engines. These sounds drew closer and closer yet no cars were visible. The noise of the engines rapidly swelled as the cars drew nearer to her whereabouts. The clamour had now reached heights that were almost deafening. Two cars appeared in her line of sight then bolted past her in quick succession, one after the other. They were moving at tremendous speed. The roar of the engines reached its peak as each car flew past, then slowly disappeared in the distance as the vehicles sped away.

Brooke saw the layout of the road before her. It was spread across two lanes on each side, divided by a tall concrete barrier down the centre, a dual carriageway. Separated by a narrow grass verge on the kerb line an adjacent footpath was also apparent on opposite sides of the carriageway. To the rear of the footpath on each side was an embankment leading up a steep hill covered in hedgerows and shrubbery. Street lights adorned and illuminated the visible length of the highway away from the roundabout, except where Brooke was stood. With a quick glance she noticed the street light immediately above her was dim, unlit, broken perhaps? In any case the dingy area in which she was standing was bought to her attention.

Something else nearby caught her by surprise. A bend in the road nearby led to a large roundabout. The layout of the road from the roundabout made her line of site limited. The sharp turn towards the roundabout meant she could only see a few metres in front. Her instincts told her this was something of further concern.

Looking up to the sky Brooke's endeavour to ascertain the time of day came unstuck. There was no sun, or even visible cloud cover. It had to be night time. All of a sudden she caught site of a figure high up. While Brooke stood on the flat surface of the pavement she could make out the suggestion of another person. The light from far away generated an almost eerie looking silouette at the peak of the steep hill on the opposite side in the distance. It appeared to be moving towards her. As the figure slowly descended the steep hill it faded into obscurity among the darkness of the hedgerows and shrubbery. Simultaneously a distant echo of a car engine started to resonate.

Engrossed in what she could see Brooke watched on with great interest as the figure clamoured down the hill. Despite her vision being obscured by darkness Brooke could just about make out plants and vegetation being trampled on and pushed to one side as the shadowy figure drew closer to the bottom. The noise of the car engine started to become more defined. The figure appeared to be stumbling as it reached the footpath. Brooke could now make out more of its defining characteristics. It appeared to be a man in a dinner jacket and smart trousers. Stumbling as he walked he appeared to be intoxicated, drunk like he had just been to a party of some sort. He appeared to be very out of place here. Did he get lost or separated from his friends or companions and why was he around these parts on his own?

With the engine noise in the distance becoming increasingly resounding the man continued to stagger towards the kerb line opposite Brooke seemingly undeterred by the clamour that was looming towards him. He looked like he was about to try and cross the street from a point immediately adjacent to the roundabout where the central barrier finished and he believed he would have an easy route without the need to walk across. At this point Brooke's instincts took over. She could foresee exactly what was going to happen. The man was about to cross the dual carriageway on a section where visibility was poor and the drivers of any oncoming vehicles pulling off the roundabout at speed would be unable to see or react to him until it was too late.

Without hesitation Brooke darted forward towards the man. She ran out into the dual carriageway on her side across the two lanes and onto his side. The speed at which she moved was phenomenal, many times faster than he was moving on his end. Once on his side of the carriageway she moved, and in those brief moments that she ran to his aid she quickly realised her predicament. She couldn't stop what was about to happen, she could only stand and observe. She then came to a sudden realisation.

What was, only moments ago the distant echo of a car engine was now a deafening bellow of disaster about to come crashing by her way with catastrophic consequences. A car flew into her view from around the corner of the roundabout. Neither the lack of visibility nor the bend on the roundabout had any impact on the ferocious speed at which the vehicle was moving. As she approached the man about to step onto the carriageway she held up both her hands with extreme defiance, one blocked his path, the other blocked that of the speeding car.

'STOP!!' she cried out, as loud as she could.

With that something happened that Brooke had not witnessed before. The drunk man in front who was about to walk into her stopped dead in his tracks, as did the car. Still in motion but motionless with one foot on the ground and the other hovering in mid-air the man was completely still. Similarly the car that was now only inches from her and the man did not move. With its lights still beaming ahead the car stood completely stationary. An immediate eerie silence fell upon the place too. The sound of wind in the trees, leaves along the ground, the footsteps of the drunk man, and not least the thundering roar of the car's engine all stopped concurrently. There was now only complete and total silence.

Brooke looked on with sheer delight and amazement. Slowly lowering her hands after a few brief seconds of cautiousness she turned to face the car in front of her. She then turned to the drunk man in front of her. Glancing down at his feet she noticed the peculiar angle of his stance due to the exact time at which she had stopped him still. Filled with excitement she could hardly contain herself. She moved from her spot and started to walk around him. As she circled round him she began to notice all the details of his appearance.

She gazed in awe at his face. He was a white middle aged man clean shaven, short brown hair with a hint of grey at the sides. His visage showed obvious signs of intoxication with blemishes, bleary green eyes and a red nose. He would otherwise have a very smart appearance were it not for him being so drunk. Everything he wore was clearly visible, an expensive tailor-made suit, a silky white shirt and shiny black shoes. Every item of clothing he had on was of the highest quality. A wealthy man no doubt, clearly in the wrong place at the wrong time.

Her dream had become like a movie that she could pause, rewind and fast forward at her will, except that she wasn't just watching her movie, she was like one of the characters in it.

Moving from her spot unhurried she started to circle round the car with great fascination. She recognised the make and model. It was a Volkswagen Golf R. Orange in colour, 3 door, 6 speed manual, shiny alloy wheels, tinted black glass windows and roof spoiler, a boy racer's car. Able to reach 154 mph flat out the vehicle was designed primarily for one reason – speed. She slowly continued to stroll around the car observing every curve and line. She crept all the way around the side of the car, past the bonnet at the rear and round the opposite side and back to the front.

The shaded design of the car windows made it impossible for her to see who was inside, although the stereo typical instincts gave her a very good idea of what they would look like. In any case that was of minor importance. Brooke's priority was to endeavour to identify her exact time and location. What's the most obvious way of telling the time? She thought to herself, and then realised all she had to do was attempt to look at the man's watch.

Approaching the figure for a second time Brooke glanced at the man's arms to see his wristwatch. The position at which the man had stopped forced his sleeves to cover his wrists and made viewing underneath them impossible. There had to be another way for her to see. She attempted to touch the man's sleeve and roll it back. This proved to be in vain.

Upon contact with the man's jacket her hand went straight through like it wasn't there. She remembered then that she was akin to a ghost in her dream. She could not change anything within it or have any physical contact with anyone, much like a movie the audience couldn't change the appearance of anything they saw in the film. All she could do essentially was fast forward and rewind, but this might be all that she needed. It dawned on her that she was able to move the events of her dream to her will. She could either go forwards or backwards.

Being only milliseconds from certain disaster for the drunk man Brooke decided that if she was going to make time move forward from this moment the outcome would be extremely graphic and distressing for her to see, even in slow motion. Brooke decided whole heartedly not to move forward with the events of her dream at this point but instead to rewind at a gradual pace in order to allow an attempt to glance at the man's watch.

She raised her hand and instinctively willed the events of her dream to rescind. To her delight everything very slowly began to move in reverse. The man started to stroll backwards at an acutely prolonged pace. The car retreated away from her at a fraction of its original speed. It was like someone had hit the rewind button one frame at a time. Brooke's attention turned primarily to the drunk man. As he slowly moved away from her she approached him closer to inspect. There had to be a moment when she could peak at his watch, she thought to herself.

As the man proceeded to back away from the roadside Brooke scrutinised his movements with great deliberation. Every motion he made, particularly with his arms was being surveyed. Brooke was determined to encounter the exact moment she needed, to grab the definitive point where his sleeves would fall back and reveal a sneak-peek at his watch. All she needed was that split second view and she could determine the exact time of the accident.

As he moved backwards at a snail's pace Brooke

continued to study the man with undivided attention just waiting for the right moment. As he continued to move she watched for several seconds then noticed him raising his arms. Instinctively slowing his movements down even more she looked at his arms with great anticipation. Her face positioned only inches away she brought time to a virtual stand-still as she observed. Brooke positioned her head sideways to peer down his sleeves. She looked down the man's left arm to determine whether he was actually wearing a watch. To her utmost discontent she saw no watch in site.

This was an enormous disappointment to her, she felt crushed. Men almost always wear their watches on their left arm. With desperate hope she suddenly realised he might be unorthodox and don it on the right instead. She changed the position of her head to peak down his right hand sleeve.

Peering through what little gap she could make out under the man's jacket Brooke managed to view a slight glimmer of something shiny in the man's sleeve. It could only be a watch. She continued to observe his motions and willed the time in her dream to accelerate higher. She then recollected that the last thing she had seen him do before he reached the pathway was raise has hand to move a tree branch in his way. This was her perfect opportunity.

The man continued to retreat away from the road-side and was quickly approaching the rear of the pavement. Sure enough his right hand slowly raised to catch the branch that stuck out behind him. It was a surreal experience for Brooke seeing this unfold in reverse. Raising his hand above his shoulder the branch suddenly flew up to the man's grip from behind his back, as if by magic. The stretching of his arm caused the man's sleeves to fall, exposing his bare, uncovered wrist watch underneath. This was Brooke's golden opportunity. Willing the time to stop at that exact moment Brooke peered forward and up at the man's watch.

The watch was a beautiful Rolex, with its face and outer rim made from solid gold and strap mixed in with silver, worth a fortune. This was just how she imagined his watch would look. Despite the man's dimly lit location Brooke was just about able to decipher the time due to the watch's gleaming design. The time read 12.11AM. This was a truly joyous moment for Brooke. She had now for the first time ever managed to find out the exact time of one of her accidents. With her intention now to just determine the exact location of the accident Brooke's attention now turned back to the road.

With time still resting on pause Brooke turned around and headed back to the roadside to truly gauge her surroundings. The biggest clues were the road signs displayed on both sides of the street.

'Kidney roundabout halfway between Borehamwood and Elstree.'

Brooke had managed to manipulate and control time in her dream and calculate the exact instance and place. She slept peacefully through the rest of the night.

CHAPTER 39

With a smile on her face Brooke slowly woke from her immersive slumber the next morning. She had two main items on her agenda today. The first was winning some money. The next was saving the man's life.

Brooke's experience of betting on horses so far was almost all theory and no practice. She had made a few flutters before in the past but these were all blind bets with her having little or no real knowledge of the horses and their previous performance. Despite her now extensive knowledge of the industry she had yet to put it to the test.

Her instincts helped her decide on where she needed to go. With the day to spare she and Ricki went to a racetrack that Brooke had picked by hand. Her gut feeling gave her the urge to pick this particular race course knowing there was something special waiting for her. They arrived early in order for Brooke to study the horses prior to the competition.

Brooke had analysed all the horses that were racing and simply had to find an unseen weakness in the bookies' analysis. A hidden sign overlooked by all the data and statistics that would give her precedence. Her intention was not to pick the strongest contender like all the bookies and make a safe bet on winning, but to see something that would give her a true advantage - a subtle factor that only she could decipher.

The first race of the day took place shortly after 1.00PM. Brooke knew the names of all the horses racing. After studying all the facts she knew the outcome. After viewing the thoroughbreds before entering the box at the start of the race she watched in undivided attention the movement of each animal, its behaviour and temperament as each was paraded before the crowds. She knew which horse would win – the favourite 'Winter Snowfall'. It was on fine physical form, with its solid track record, not to mention a good rapport with the jockey. They clearly knew each other, working together a long time and this was one of the most underrated signs of a winner. She could have bet but even the best bookies' odds at 1 in 3 were far too small for Brooke. Sure she could bet on it and make herself a tidy sum but she wanted to wait until just the right moment. She wanted to wait for her golden opportunity to bet on a name with odds so ridiculous that she would make a fortune if she predicted it correctly. Besides which she wanted to be as discreet as possible which would not be possible if she mysteriously won every race. She was being extremely patient and calculated.

Brooke and Ricki sat at the front of the crowd and watched as the horse came in just as Brooke had foreseen.

Brooke studied the information for the next race. She observed the horses before the race once again and spotted the favourite - 'Brown Destroyer' - a fitting name for such a horse. This horse rarely lost a race at this track, and when it did it was a close call. She once again knew what the outcome would be and could have made a bet again but the potential rewards were too small. She continued to wait patiently for the perfect moment.

The next few races took place with Brooke and Ricki watching from the front of the crowd.

'When are you gonna make a bet?' Ricki asked her repeatedly. To which she insistently replied by telling her to be patient.

'You knew what was gonna happen in both those races. You knew which horse was going to win didn't you?' said Ricki. 'How did you do it?' she added.

'I don't really know' replied Brooke. 'I mean I study the facts and statistics and I observe the horses before they race. From that I just know the outcome'. she added.

'So what are we waiting for now?' asked Ricki.

'We just sit here and wait for the right moment.' replied Brooke. 'I've got a feeling I'm looking for a sign and I'll know exactly when that happens' She added.

'Did you bring some money to bet?' asked Brooke.

'Yes I bought my life savings, all £117 of it!' joked Ricki. 'Let me know when you're on it and I'll be right behind you! Did you bring any? she asked.

'Just a bit' replied Brooke looking somewhat dismissive.

Over the course of the next few hours the two sisters continued to watch the races. Ricki enjoyed several large glasses of white wine while Brooke, wanting to remain entirely sober and focused on what she was doing, drank only fruit juice and water.

Now on to their seventh race since they arrived Brooke was all too familiar with the statistics. She watched as they marched them out. The favourite was one 'Rapid Waterfall' but it's persona didn't excite Brooke. One horse caught her eye - 'Volcanic Ashley'. She had read about her before. Statistically this steed was weak. It had never won a single race yet Brooke knew there was far more to studying any horse than simply reading its history in numbers and letters. This particular quadroped had been the victim of very unfortunate circumstances in its past. Brooke knew this was one to watch.

Brooke looked on as the animal was strolled along the track side. The favourite followed closely behind. Brooke analysed and compared the behaviour and demeanour of both gallopers. Their conduct caught Brooke's attention with great intrigue. She noticed subtle if somewhat clear differences in their behaviour and movement. Firstly the jockey riding the favourite was different to the usual rider, the same hoop who had won almost every single race previously. He was noticeably bigger than the other horseman. Perhaps the usual jockey was off sick or injured. In any case even after 'weighing out' before the race in order to balance the load the jockey's mass can still have an effect on the horse's performance. In this case the difference was quite significant. Judging by how far his body was angled over the top of the horse while leaning forward Brooke determined approximately five inches difference in height. Coupled with disparity in build between the two jockeys Brooke estimated the overall weight variation to be between nine and ten pounds.

This factor in itself was not enough to change the outcome of the race but Brooke was observant of additional aspects. The favourite horse was fast but had a relatively low Horse Racing Rating when compared to most others in the race – it hadn't won as many races. The statistics also revealed that all races won by this horse in the past were on soft ground. That day the weather was hot and sunny. The weather outlook for several days previously had been dry. The brown and withered grass indicated that the ground was arid and thirsty for moisture. Brooke also observed a slight limp on the leg of the favourite steed. The arduous pressure felt with each step on the firm soil of the course was clearly causing pain. Perhaps an abscess had recently appeared on its hoof - a common injury for thoroughbreds.

The horse was generally restless too. Perhaps the hot, dry weather had affected the animal's sleep. The jockey's attempts to calm the steed had little success. He did not have the apparent rapport that the previous rider enjoyed.

Brooke's attention now turned back to the underdog of the race – Volcanic Ashley. Her persona was the mirror opposite to the favourite, as was much of her statistical data. Almost all of the previous races it had lost were on soft ground, and today the ground was hard. The steed's expression, posture and movement all showed positive signs. Exhibiting alertness and interest at what was in front, her ears were pointed forward. Chewing her mouth with her head lowered she gave off the notion of feeling good. Brooke knew this horse was her winner.

CHAPTER 40

Leaning in to towards Ricki Brooke pointed at Volcanic Ashley while whispering in her sister's ear.

'That's our horse' she murmured.

'Which one?' asked Ricki, with anticipation.

'Number eleven - Volcanic Ashley' replied Brooke.

Shocked at her sister's remark Ricki's face turned to a look of total astoundment.

'What!!?' replied Ricki. 'That's the least likely to win out of all of them. It's never won a race before and it's got the lowest odds of any horse we've seen today! What makes you think that's gonna win!?' she insisted.

'I'm just getting a good vibe coming from it' replied Brooke. 'Everything about her body language is saying we're onto a winner. The favourite must have got out of bed the wrong side this morning and so did the jockey. It looks weak and restless and so do all the others by comparison. I'm telling you this is a dead cert'. she added.

Won over by her sister's explanation Ricki asked

Brooke to put on a bet for her and gave her the money while she went to the bar. Brooke approached the betting counter and after queuing for a short time put Ricki's money down as well as a certain sum of her own for Volcanic Ashley to win. The lady at the counter gazed back stunned at the amount she put down. After being given her betting tickets Brooke met with Ricki back at the side of the track where she handed Ricki hers.

'Thanks' replied Ricki while handing Brooke her drink. 'How much did you bet?' she added.

At that point a voice was heard over the loudspeaker announcing that the race was about to start. Both sisters' attention turned to the horses as they entered the starting gates. Ricki leaned over and whispered to Brooke.

'You realise if you're wrong about this you're never gonna hear the last of it from me!?' she murmured.

Responding to her sister Brooke turned to Ricki and smiled. 'In about two minutes time I'll be accepting your apology!' she bragged.

Re-assured by Brooke's comment Ricki was now quietly confident in her sister's prediction. The volume of footfalls soon escalated as crowds gathered round for the start of the race. The horn for the start of the race blared out over the loudspeaker and no sooner had the starting gates opened than the horses bolted out onto the track.

As each of the twelve steeds emerged the sight at first glance was too much to decipher. After an initial scurry the favourite – Rapid Waterfall could be seen gaining lead among all the others, including Volcanic Ashley. The two sisters watched on with extreme anticipation as they listened to the commentator's voice;

'And after a confusing start we see Rapid Waterfall take first place as we reach the end of the first furlong. With Son-block 2010 in second place and Rocket Roy in third. Near the back of the pack, not surprisingly is Volcanic Ashley, still yet to win a race. Rapid Waterfall steaming on ahead with his replacement jockey in the rider's seat. Positions remain unchanged as we near the end of the second furlong now.'

Ricki gazed on the whole event with a sense of dread. That money Brooke put down for her was the last of her capital. She had no other cash, nor any way of making more in the near future. Their horse was trailing behind with only seconds to go before the end of the competition. Reacting in dire fright she began to bury her face in her hands. Covering her eyes with her head arched to the ground her hopes were crushed. How could her sister be wrong about this? What the hell was she thinking, betting on a horse with such a poor history of performance?

Acknowledging her sister's behaviour Brooke's attention turned to Ricki for a short time.

'Trust me' she insisted as she slapped her on the back.

Brooke remained confident that events would turn around. Unbeknown to Ricki this affair had panned out exactly as Brooke anticipated, and the race was not over yet. With undivided attention she continued to observe the full events of the race unfold as the commentator persevered with every detail he sighted, bellowing out through the loudspeaker with increased noise. Turning once again to Ricki Brooke began to whisper in her ear.

'Watch the horse in front' she murmured.

At that point certain events took a turn for the unexpected. Exhibiting some evident signs the steed in first place – Rapid Waterfall began to slow down. The demeanour given by the horse that Brooke observed before the race was starting to reveal itself. The animal was losing ground over the horses behind it. Reacting to the quadroped's notable shift in performance the jockey began to beat the animal repeatedly with his cain. This only had an adverse effect on Rapid Waterfall's performance. The animal continued to slow as the other racers began to catch up. Perhaps the horse's apparent leg injury, exacerbated by solid ground and hot sunny weather, coupled with the inexperienced rider were now starting to take their toll.

In contrast the events nearer the back of the race

were simultaneously beginning to alter. Giving the other horses room to breath, the open air of the extended race course allowed the other steeds the space they needed away from the other contenders. The obstacles caused by the presence of other racers were now beginning to dissipate and all horses and riders instinctively found their place among the others as they dashed up the track. After a slow start caused largely by the hindrance of other animals in her way, their horse Volcanic Ashley started to find her footing. Successfully navigating away from the pack she and the jockey now made the perfect team. The demeanour they gave off before the race was beginning to shine through and as the pair of them began to pick up pace the announcer became hysterical with his findings at what was unfolding on the track. A race that showed this level of transformation was a rare occurrence.

As both sisters observed all events of the race unfold Ricki's fear now quickly turned to excitement and as the loudspeaker bellowed out with increasing intensity the noise of the crowd quickly became a resounding clamour of excited commotion. They all watched on and listened as the commentator continued;

'It appears that events have taken a turn for the worse for Number twelve Rapid Waterfall who appears to be slowing down. The other horses have picked up pace. He's losing ground on all of them. He's level with num-

ber eight Sunblock 2010 who has now overtaken him. Number eight Sunblock 2010 is now in the lead as we approach the fifth furlong. At the back of the race we see number eleven Volcanic Ashley break away from the rest of them and is now gaining traction up the field. She has already overtaken most of the others is now almost level with third place number five Rocket Roy. Number twelve Rapid Waterfall's speed appears to still be declining as he is neck and neck with number eleven and number five. The favourite appears to be in trouble now as number eleven Volcanic Ashley dashes ahead. Who could have possibly predicted this unlikely turn of events. Number eight Sunblock 2010 remains in the lead as number eleven Volcanic Ashley is now closely behind in second. The two of them are now neck and neck as we approach the finish line. Both horses determined to reach it first it appears that number eleven Volcanic Ashley has taken the lead as both horses cross the line. What a race this has been. Number eleven Volcanic Ashley has taken the lead. I repeat number eleven Volcanic Ashley, the true underdog of the horse racing world has taken the lead and landed first place in this truly historic race!'

Witnessing the whole ordeal from start to finish the two sisters were in a state of unimaginable excitement and happiness, the extent of which neither had ever felt. Looking at each other they screamed and cheered upon hearing the commentator's voice and witnessing the outcome. Throwing their arms up as they yelled out they then hugged each other in celebration. The sheer noise and thrill of their commemoration between themselves was so conspicuous that it drew the attention of the entire crowd. Seeing the obvious reasons for their delight spectators all around looked on as they cheered.

Wiping away their tears after the initial excitement several minutes passed and the commotion around them eventually died down.

'How much have I won?' asked Ricki.

'Well I put your bet down of £117 which at odds of 100:1 means you win exactly £11,700' replied Brooke.

'Ha ha ha!!!' laughed Ricki with disbelief. 'I'm rich beyond my wildest dreams!' she exclaimed.

'So how much have you won' she asked Brooke.

'Let's go and claim our winnings shall we!?' she replied.

'Brooke....why do you keep avoiding my question!?' asked Ricki with suspicion and intrigue. 'Exactly how much money did you bet?' she added.

Brooke looked back at her with an arkward smile.

'Well you know I had a little pot of money left over for my savings, I might have just done the silly thing and put it all down on the horse to win' she replied

'What!? That must have been about ten grand in total!' Insisted Ricki.

'Well actually it was more like twenty five' confessed Brooke.

'Twenty five grand!?' exclaimed Ricki. 'You're telling me that you just put down twenty five grand on a horse with odds of 100:1! That must mean you've won £250,000!' she added.

'Err....no' replied Brooke 'It means I've just won £2.5 million'.

'Oh my god!!' replied Ricki. 'We're rich. We are like...set up for life!' she added.

'What's all this 'we'?' replied Brooke with a smug grin. 'This is my money!' she added.

Shocked at her sister's response Ricki looked at her in disbelief.

'Hey you gotta share some with me!' insisted Ricki.

As the two of them continued to argue they started to make their way inside to collect their winnings. Upon entering the door to the main building the other punters inside turned around and a large cheer erupted all around them. They had already become famous for their lucky gamble.

After approaching the counter, they handed over their receipts and bank details. A few minutes passed and their winnings were transferred to their accounts. Before leaving the race track £2,511,700 richer the sisters ordered a taxi to pick them up outside the main entrance and went home safe, without delay. Mission accomplished.

CHAPTER 41

The two sisters arrived back home, almost too excited for words! They stepped out the taxi giggling like little girls as they quietly discussed their plans for using the money.

'Let's go out and celebrate!' said Ricki. 'We could book a table at the nicest restaurant in London, or even better we could go out shopping up West. Just think about it – shoes, handbags, jewelry. We could have it all!' she added.

'I'd like to buy the essential things first, like the equipment we need for our little project, and let's not forget we have somewhere we need to be tonight!' insisted Brooke as she approached the house to unlock the front door.

After the excitement they had that day they had both forgotten the real reason why they were doing this in the first place.

'Yes there'll be plenty of time for that!' replied Ricki. 'Why don't we go out and have some fun!?' she told her.

'Well I suppose it wouldn't hurt' replied Brooke as

they walked inside.

They began discussing in more detail their intentions of spending the money and by the time they had settled in at home Ricki already had it planned out in her mind, as had Brooke yet their ideas were somewhat different and clearly reflected their contrasting personalities. Ricki wanted to spend the money on everything she had ever wanted, whereas Brooke was cautious and calculated. She thought more about what she needed, not what she wanted. Regardless the two of them both decided to treat the rest of their day as a celebration.

The two sisters freshened up, changed their casual clothes to some more suitable attire then left the house. They enjoyed the rest of the afternoon browsing around the upper market fashion retailers around Regents Street and Knightsbridge, then after being exhausted from all their retail therapy, enjoyed an expensive meal together at a top restaurant in Mayfair. They arrived home late that night, but not too late for their appointment.

CHAPTER 42

Still exhilarated from their electrifying day the two sisters booked a taxi to the location in Brooke's dream. The place where the man was run over by a car, late at night - Kidney roundabout halfway between Borehamwood and Elstree. Brooke knew the drive would be approximately 45 minutes from where she lived, if there was little or no traffic. This was one substantial advantage of driving at this time – the roads were quiet. She took no chances in any case and left two hours before it was due to start. Brooke used the GPS function on her mobile phone to pinpoint the exact location to be dropped off. The taxi driver was as reluctant to stop as he was puzzled by her unusual request, yet eventually gave in when Brooke offered to pay double for what was already a lucrative journey for him.

Arriving one hour and forty minutes early to their location they exited the taxi by the roadside near to the roundabout. After giving the taxi driver explicit instructions to collect them from that same location after exactly two hours and not a minute earlier, Brooke offered him £50. Tearing the note in half she promised him the other piece on condition that he carried out her request exactly as she had asked. Unhappy at committing the unlawful act of disfiguring a bank note she knew it was for a good reason. She and her sister did not long for the peril of being left there at night with no means of travelling home, and besides which the wrongdoing of her crime paled into insignificance to saving a man's life.

Knowing how early they were the two sisters decided to sit down on a wall conveniently located near the impending crash site. With time on their hands they began discussing their eventful day as well as detailing their plans for the future.

'How much did we spend today?' asked Ricki 'About £10 grand!?' she added.

'No it's more like £21,940, including what I've paid the cabby' replied Brooke.

'I think mum and dad would be really proud' insisted Ricki.

'What! Of spending over £20,000 grand on crap we don't need!?' replied Brooke sarcastically.

'No!!' insisted Ricki. 'For using your brain and winning all that money!' she added.

Chuckling away Brooke remained silent.

'We need to set up some kind of base of operations' Brooke then announced.

'What? Like a batcave!?' joked Ricki.

'In a manner of speaking' replied Brooke. 'But a batcave without bats that's not a cave!' she added. 'We'll need somewhere private and secluded but also with good transport links in every direction' she continued.

Peering around for the drunk man to somehow magically appear early Ricki with eagerness, then veered towards Brooke.

'How long have we got now before he arrives?' she asked.

'About one hour and 38 minutes' replied Brooke quite abruptly.

The two of them continued to sit there in the calm dead of night with just the odd car flying past every few minutes being the only other contact with the outside world they had witnessed. Otherwise they spent most of their time discussing what properties to purchase while perusing websites on their phones for ideas.

With time racing past quite rapidly the moment they had sought was now quickly approaching. Only minutes away from witnessing the tragic moment the two of them began to discuss their plan.

'Right' declared Brooke. 'We both know what we need to do just as we discussed. All we have to do is stop him walking into the road at the precise time that the car drives past' she added.

'Should be simple enough' replied Ricki.

Several more minutes passed and it was almost time. Eager and determined the two of them stood up ready for action. Peering up they observed a shadowy figure appear above the bank that towered over the roadside. It was the drunk man, just as Brooke witnessed in her dream. The distant roar of the oncoming car could be heard as the man emerged and started to hike down the slope.

They began to walk closer to the spot of the accident when all of a sudden something disastrous occurred. Lying along the width of the footpath was a slippery wet puddle of mud on an otherwise dry pavement. It had encroached onto the footpath from the vegetation at the back, most likely caused by footfalls or vehicles driving on and off the path and landscape. Marching along the outer side of the path and unable to see the obstruction in front of her Brooke stood on the mud and slipped to the side. The force of her tumble made her crash against Ricki. With a scream and a gasp the two of them fell sideways uncontrollably into the adjacent shrubbery. With the man continuing his descent down the hill only seconds away from disaster the two sisters laid in a heap as the sound of the oncoming vehicle drew closer.

Once again they had to act fast if they wanted

to save this man's life. Lying on top of her sister Brooke stumbled unwieldy to her feet then tried to move forward while calling out to the man just metres away from them. Her attempt was in vain. She slipped once again on the wet grass and vegetation that surrounded them and fell on her face. Persisting with his trek towards the road the man seemed oblivious to their horseplay. The rustling noise of the surrounding leaves coupled with the man's drunken disposition made the commotion of their situation difficult to capture his attention. Were it not such a serious situation they were in these events could easily be seen as comical.

It was now Ricki's turn. Less hindered by the shrubbery she simultaneously stood up and dashed forward. Having now reached the bottom of the slope the man found himself in recognisable view. His identity was unmistakable. A smartly dressed middle aged man in a tailor made suit, white shirt and black shoes. Clean shaven, short brown hair with a hint of grey at the sides, having clear signs of intoxication.

Ricki saw him approach the footpath and about to cross the road. With the noise of the car becoming more resounding she was lucky enough not to slip as she ran towards the man as fast as she could. With her arms out she dashed towards him. Screaming in distress she quickly approached the drunk, and with hands wrapped firmly around his waist she squeezed as hard as she could. Pushing up against him her determined momentum forced the two of them to the ground along the footpath as the car flew past the three of them.

Lying on the ground once again Ricki lay on top of the man just inches away from certain death. The deafening noise of the car in front coupled with a strange young lady on top of him left the man completely startled. Who was this young lady and why was she here? Where did that car come from and would it have hit him had he not been stopped? The two sisters' tension quickly receded as soon as the car drove past and the noise of the vehicle faded in the distance.

They had saved the man's life. Walking towards the two of them on the floor Brooke began to explain the situation to the drunk man as she helped them both to their feet.

Still baffled by the abnormal turn of events the man thanked the two of them and continued on his journey. He proceeded to cross the street as originally intended, though this time not endangered by oncoming cars. The two sisters watched as he reached the other side, then up the grassy hill opposite he soon disappeared into the night. Brooke and Ricki then turned to each other and let out a huge sigh of relief.

'That was too close!' exclaimed Ricki.

'Tell me about it' replied Brooke.

Dusting themselves off of mud and dirt as best they could the two of them sat back on the wall as before and waited for their taxi to return. Their ride arrived on time and after giving being taken back home Brooke gave the driver the other side of the £50 note she had promised earlier. The taxi driver expressed curiousness on the events of their trip and the reason why their clothes were soiled, to which they both replied that they 'fell-over'.

Drained from their long day of saving lives, horse racing and hauling all their shopping bags the two ladies barely even studied their fine wares they bought earlier. They agreed to go straight to bed with barely a word spoken between them.

The more coordinated of the two sisters, Brooke hit the sack first and immediately descended into an intense slumber. Climbing in to her own bed Ricki followed soon after and she too fell immediately into tranquility.

CHAPTER 43

A blurry image appeared. It was dark and gloomy. Shadowy with textures and outlines overlapping. Brooke was back in her dream state. She was alone in a small, narrow enclosure – a tunnel of some kind. The tunnel was lit up, but at the same time quite dark and dingy with it's only radiance of glow being somewhat inadequate. Brooke turned herself all around to observe her surroundings. She could make out concrete lining the floors and ceilings of the tunnel. Multi-coloured graffiti overlaid the walls with hideous effect. Rarely had she seen so much tagging in one place, most of which was illegible. Brooke could hear the rumble of vehicles driving past above her head as the noise echoed through the tunnel. She observed steps and a ramp at each end heading up. She was standing in a subway.

Brooke wasted no further time. She moved towards one end of the subway, the one slightly closer to her whereabouts and listened with anticipation for anything interesting or unusual. Approaching the exit she could soon view the steps and ramp leading up. She saw nothing, just an empty walkway. What she could hear however was clear and distinct noises from above. The bustle of ongoing traffic that was all too familiar was operating over her. Brooke immediately acknowledged that it was night time with visibility made possible from street lights and glare from windows. Moving closer to the sound she ascended the stairs away from the tunnel to be met with an energetic view.

She was at a busy road junction, a roundabout with exits in all directions. Road accidents were already becoming a thorn in her side and she had a feeling something big was about to happen again. She could see traffic building up on all sides leading into the roundabout and cars speeding off on the opposite sides leading away. Traffic in the lanes leading into the roundabout was typical. As with most they split in two. In the left the cars were turning left and going straight ahead. In the right they were obviously turning right. Observing the view before her Brooke scrutinized every detail. She viewed several pedestrians on the opposite side of the street, all marching away from her location. They carried on pacing away from the roundabout and eventually out of sight. They were irrelevant. She knew that whoever was involved was going to be someone moving towards this place, or at this location already. Peering around behind her for more potential victims she saw nothing. The footways were clear, for now.

Remembering her abilities and what she had now learned to do in her dreams she decided to levitate off the ground in order to improve her sight. Raising herself upwards she now floated six feet higher. Her new position gave her an excellent landscape view of the whole junction. She could now see everything. At first sight nothing caught her attention. As traffic flowed past she continued to watch and observe. Catching her attention someone began to approach the roundabout diagonally opposite her side of the street. Appearing to be in a rush it was a young brunette haired lady in jeans and t-shirt. As she drew nearer to Brooke she made regular glances across the road, looking backwards and forwards at the traffic flows she clearly wanted to cross. Ignoring the obvious signs for the pedestrian subway she obviously had no time in her mind to take the safe option. Instead she was willing to risk her own life to shave precious seconds off her journey time.

Now well aware of the drill Brooke observed the young lady with much anticipation. Knowing she was about to make a big mistake and pay the ultimate price Brooke looked on as the lady moved out on to the road. With vehicles on the inside lane currently stationary the lady decided to cross but was unaware of the approaching cars on the outside. Oblivious to her own danger the lady stepped into the outside lane as a vehicle approached at speed from out of nowhere.

Knowing the outcome Brooke decided to act quickly. She held up her hand as she had done before.

'STOP!' she yelled out.

The whole roundabout came to an abrupt halt. All noises and sounds ceased instantly and there became an eerie silence. Cars stood still with their lights still beaming ahead while drivers behind the wheels sat motionless. Inches away from the car about to hit her, the young lady stood still on one foot staring ahead at the opposite side of the street, blissfully unaware that she was not about to reach it.

Impressed at what she had made occur for the second time in her dreams Brooke now had to decipher the exact time and place in order to ensure it was prevented. Glancing at the buildings all around her one that caught her eye was a notably large one just a few hundred metres from her location. A large sign on the side of the building said Kingston Hospital. Being welcome news to Brooke this landmark obviously made her location considerably easier to find.

Knowing that now all she needed was the time she looked all around her for any clocks visible from the street. No such luck. Where else could she find out she wondered? With a moments thought she realised she could view a clock from a dashboard on one of the nearby cars. Deciding to float back to earth and approach the nearest car to her she attempted to glance through the passenger window. The glare on the outside of the vehicle however, coupled with poor visibility on the inside made it impossible for Brooke to view the clock.

Deciding to try another car Brooke strolled over to the one behind and once again decided to attempt a glance through the passenger window at the dashboard. Due to the position of the car and the inside readings being well illuminated she was able to view the clock quite clearly. The time on the digital display read 12:10. Being at night it was clearly ten minutes after midnight.

Feeling content with the relative ease of her findings Brooke forced herself to wake from her dream and note the findings on her phone. After jotting down the words subway, roundabout, Kingston Hospital and 12.10AM on the notes page of her mobile she settled back in bed and slept soundly until morning.

CHAPTER 44

Brooke woke from sleeping but felt an intense discomfort across her head. The irritation was that of a throbbing headache, quite unlike what she had sensed before. Dozing in bed she lay awake but with her eyes firmly closed pondering the possible cause of her soreness. Was she hungover from the alcohol she drank yesterday? She had been drinking but not too excessively, or at least that's what she and her sister thought. Was it an allergic reaction of some kind? She had not eaten or drunk anything recently that she didn't have before when she was well. Was it because of stress? She had been under a lot of stress for weeks now but this was the first time she'd felt anguish like this. She continued to reflect on her condition for several minutes before finally budging from her bedstead.

Disoriented and still in pain she shuffled herself towards the bathroom. Opening the toiletry cabinet she aggressively reached for her paracetamol pills. In doing so she stroked her hand past other bottles and packaging either side which fell over.

One small box cascaded down on to the sink with a resounding racket that echoed through the room. Indifferent to the trivial disarray of toiletries and the sudden clamour of plastic falling on to the ceramic surface Brooke continued un-phased. She didn't care. Her only concern was relieving the unceasing pain of her headache.

After filling a beaker half way from the tap she ripped a pill from the packet, swigged a mouthful of water then swallowed. She then tore off another pill. Popping it in to her mouth she guzzled more water then swallowed again. She repeated this process twice more – four pills in total, double the recommended dosage. Taking a deep breath she rested on the toilet seat, hands on her head. Believing the cause of her discomfort might be due to dehydration she filled another beaker with water then quaffed it down. Still not satisfied she filled another beaker and drank it.

Being woken up from all the commotion Ricki peered round the open bathroom door. 'What's that noise?' she asked.

'Got a terrible headache, just took some pills' replied Brooke.

Rising to her feet she stood up and staggered out the bathroom door, past Ricki and back to her bedroom. Looking on at her sister Ricki watched with concern.

'Can I help with anything?' she asked.

'No thanks' replied Brooke. 'Going back to bed now' she added.

CHAPTER 45

Several hours passed and Brooke remained in bed. Lying awake for much of the time she failed to shift the relentless hurt she felt from her continuous headache. The pills she swallowed earlier did little to numb the pain. She eventually decided to get up. Ignoring the relentless irritation Brooke powered through her soreness and discomfort as best she could. She showered, got dressed then went to the kitchen for coffee and a snack. Preparing her late morning drink before pouring out a large mug full she uncharacteristically added two spoonfuls of sugar. Perhaps that might help? She thought. After sipping a quick mouthful of coffee she grabbed a chocolate bar from her cupboard then entered the living room where Ricki was sat watching TV.

'Still got that bad headache?' she asked.

'Yeah' replied Brooke nodding her head gently. Moving slowly Brooke sat down gently on the sofa next to Ricki who watched on with great interest. She began to talk.

'Why don't we....'

'No I don't want to' declared Brooke before Ricki could finish her sentence.

'How did you...'

'I know what you were gonna say before you did' replied Brooke as she interrupted her once again.

'You don't know what I was gonna suggest!' insisted Ricki.

'Yes I do' replied Brooke.

'You were gonna suggest going for a walk in the park' she added.

Shocked and surprised at her sister's response Ricki continued. 'How did you know!?' she asked.

'I just know what you're gonna say before you do' Brooke replied.

With Ricki unsure of what else to say the two sisters continued to sit on the sofa for several minutes longer, Ricki watching TV in shock and Brooke with head still in hands. Deciding to finally speak she looked over at Ricki.

'Maybe you're right' she declared. 'Maybe I should go out. The exercise and fresh air might do me some good and help my head'.

'Great!' replied Ricki. 'I'll come too' she added.

Finishing her coffee and snack Brooke slowly stood up and got ready to leave the house. Ricki followed and assisted with her empty cup and rubbish. They grabbed their belongings and headed out. They walked out the property and on to the street. The nearest park they liked was five minutes walk from their house. Initially empty of people Brooke strolled with relative ease up the street, albeit at a significantly reduced pace she wasn't completely unhindered by her pain. Nevertheless she was determined to battle through and try to enjoy herself.

'I meant to say to you also about my latest dream last night. I've got details about the time and place of the next accident....' declared Brooke.

As she began to explain further something else caused her a considerable distraction. Peering ahead Brooke's voice went silent as she witnessed someone walk towards them down the street. It was a dark-haired middle aged woman in a red coat. Nothing was out of the ordinary about her to the average person yet the sight of her was clearly a grave concern to Brooke.

'Oh my god!' she blurted out.

Collapsing to the floor she held her head in her hands screaming in pain, as if she was being tortured. Lying on the ground of the pavement she began to shiver and wince at the same time. Looking on in horror and disbelief Ricki tried to assist her.

'What's wrong!?' she asked her with extreme worry and distress.

Remaining unresponsive to her sister's questions Brooke stayed incapacitated on the ground and persisted to scream in pain.

'What's wrong!!?' asked Ricki again with even more insistence. Becoming emotional at her sister's predicament she persevered with communicating with her. 'You're scaring me!' she exclaimed.

Her condition remaining unchanged Brooke continued to scream in pain as Ricki watched on helplessly. Nearing their location the woman caught site of the commotion and walked closer to where the two sisters had stopped with the same shock as what befell Ricki.

Approaching them both the woman in red spoke. 'Is your friend OK?' she asked Ricki.

'I don't know what's wrong with her!' replied Ricki hysterically. 'She just fell to the ground and started screaming.

The woman stood over Brooke and addressed her directly. 'Are you alright my dear, what's wrong?'

For the first time since catching site of the lady Brooke reacted. Waving her hand very dismissively she thoroughly avoided any eye contact with the lady.

'Go away!' she yelled with her face still touching the floor. The woman's face turned to a look of horror as Ricki acknowledged what Brooke had told her and decided to act.

'Yes please do as she says and just walk away' Ricki told the lady. 'I'm sorry' she added.

Shocked and confused at this bizarre turn of events the lady reluctantly turned and walked off just as she had been instructed.

As the lady marched away Brooke became less agitated. Her screaming became slowly quieter and she gradually became more settled. After a short time she became silent and still on the ground. Looking on Ricki crouched back down beside her.

'Are you better now?' she asked her.

'I think so' replied Brooke.

'You scared the crap out of me, what the hell just happened to you!?' asked Ricki.

'You just fell to the ground and started screaming'.

'I couldn't help it' replied Brooke. 'I just felt overcome with pain as soon as I saw that lady, it was like my headache increased by about 1000%'.

'But why?' replied Ricki. 'She didn't even do anything'.

'I know' replied Brooke. 'But I looked at her and saw her whole life flash before my eyes. I've never met her before but I know just about everything about her. She's 45 years old, married with two teenage girls and she works at the stock exchange. She catches the 08.14 train to London every morning. She likes Indian takeaway and drinking Prosecco. She plays squash every Friday night with her best friend.'

Astounded at the level she had rarely known before Ricki was once again in disbelief at what she heard.

'How the hell do you know all this?' she asked her.

'I'm not entirely sure' replied Brooke. 'It's like I just took one look at her and everything about her just got wrapped in a ball and thrown at my head like a bomb!'

Having recovered somewhat from her ordeal Ricki helped Brooke to her feet.

'Do you still want to go for a walk?' she asked her.

'Yes I feel better now' replied Brooke.

Continuing their walk up the street Ricki turned to Brooke and spoke. 'You really scared me there' she said. 'I hope I never have to see that happen again' she added.

'I hope so too' replied Brooke.

Approaching a junction someone else came in to their view. Hesitant, Ricki's attention turned to Brooke as the person drew nearer to the two of them. It was a smartly dressed middle aged man wearing a suit and tie. Upon clear site of the man's face Brooke quickly became somewhat distressed again. Ceasing to a halt she once again held her hands to her head as the pain became more intense. The severe trauma she'd experienced just moments earlier had begun again.

'Oh my god!' she yelled. 'My head!'

Acknowledging her sister's reaction Ricki decided this time to be far more decisive.

'Fight it Brooke, try to control the pain like you have with everything else. Remember you're the one in control' she told her.

'It's so painful!' exclaimed Brooke. 'It's like another bomb's gone off in my head'. Desperate and determined to help her sister Ricki persisted with her advice.

'Try to focus' she told her.

Recognising her sister's advice Brooke decided to act on it. Unlike last time she had already remained on her feet which in-itself was a good start. Her head facing down with eyes shut she clenched her fists tightly in front of herself in concentration. The man approaching them drew even closer to the point he noticed the curious behaviour of the two sisters, though he did not deem it serious enough for him to stop and offer assistance.

Becoming less irritable Brooke was able to compose herself more as he came closer. Holding out her hand while facing down at the ground as he walked passed she gently grasped his arm and spoke.

'You're gonna win I promise you!' she told him.

With his face immediately transformed to an air of astoundment the man appeared mystified at first then almost immediately seemed to acknowledge what she said. His first instinct would be to stop and ask her what she meant but part of him appeared not to want to challenge her advice. Clearly affected by what Brooke had told him he continued on his way and soon disappeared out of site of the two sisters.

Unmoved from the spot where she was standing Brooke now appeared to be somewhat recovered from her former discomfort. Ricki had a better understanding of her predicament too.

'Did you see that guy's life as well?' she asked her 'What is it you said he was gonna win?' she added. Looking up at her Brooke replied. 'The fight of his life'.

After watching the man's image fade in the distance they turned and walked on. Continuing their stroll along the footpath Brooke began to speak to Ricki.

'That was good advice you gave me about trying to control the pain' she said to her.

'Do you feel better now then?' asked Ricki.

'A little' she replied. 'My headache doesn't feel so intense now'.

The two sisters continued along the street and were nearing the end when they caught site of someone else as they exited from an adjacent subway. It was a young mother carrying a carrier bag full of groceries and a small child, whose face was buried in her mother's shoulder. Upon sight of the woman's face Brooke's reaction was intense. She felt the sharp pain in her head increase significantly, albeit less so than with previous encounters. Now able to endure walking with her discomfort Brooke was managing better than before. Approaching the young mother their manner became visible to her. Her head bowed down avoiding eye contact as she drew nearer the lady Brooke pointed at her while they walked passed and spoke.

'You forget the butter' she told her.

As the two sisters strolled on the lady stopped and turned towards her baffled and confused at first but then seemed to acknowledge what she'd said. Remaining speechless she stood her small child down and began searching through the groceries in her shopping bag. She realised that Brooke was indeed correct.

'How did you know that' asked Ricki.

'I don't know' replied Brooke. It's just like I saw her face and her file downloaded itself into my head all at once'.

'And that was all you had to tell her, that she'd

forgotten the butter!? Wasn't there anything more important you could say to her!?' exclaimed Ricki.

'That was all she needed to know for now!' insisted Brooke.

'Not everyone's life is in imminent danger' she laughed.

Shocked at Brooke's change in mood Ricki let out a stress-relieving laugh with her sister. They continued to chuckle away for some distance after which they approached a bend in the road. With her headaches beginning to dwindle coupled with her continuous laughter Brooke's mood began to greatly improve. She was once again more optimistic about her situation.

As they turned the corner Brooke's mood very quickly turned sour. The sight before her was that of a very crowded retail area. Faces of pedestrians could be seen everywhere traversing each other in all directions. People of all ages and backgrounds could be seen standing and talking, walking and talking, staring at window displays, delivering goods and crossing the street. Some were smartly dressed, others were scruffy. They were young and old alike. Ricki and Brooke both should have anticipated this before.

The view immediately proved too much for Brooke to handle. Upon sight of the crowd Brooke reacted overwhelmingly troubled. Whereas before she had faced just one person at a time she now faced over a hundred. Glancing at everyone's faces within her field of vision she gasped in horror. Instinctively backing away from where she had just come she yelled out in pain. The agony was pure torture. As she moved away Ricki attempted to assist.

'Keep it under control' she urged her.

Neglecting what Ricki tried to say to her Brooke continued backwards around the corner while facing forwards with her head in her hands like before. Behind her was a flight of steps that led down to the subway. Oblivious to her own location Brooke stubbornly continued to edge closer to the steps while facing away from them. Ricki persisted in her attempts to try and assist Brooke with her suffering.

'Remember to try and focus' she told her.

With her torturous discomfort reaching new heights that she had never experienced before these attempts proved in vain as Brooke advanced closer still to the flight of steps behind her.

Having now become more aware of Brooke's imminent mortal danger in addition to her extreme discomfort and agony Ricki also noticed her movement towards the subway was becoming a major concern.

'Mind the steps behind you!' she cried.

Still unmindful of her imminent peril Brooke relented with walking away without due care and attention. Upon realisation of her sister's very real danger and her apparent disobedience of her instructions Ricki tried to advance towards Brooke in an attempt to physically restrain her.

Her valiant attempt at saving her sister failed. As Brooke put her last foot down to what she thought was the ground she tumbled backwards down the steep flight of steps overlooking the subway. As she descended backwards her whole body weight forced her to twist awkwardly. Hitting her head on the cold metal lining of the footstep the loud crack of her skull was heard being fractured, followed by the splitting noise of her broken leg bone against the hard, uneven surface as she rolled down the stairs unconscious and landed at the bottom. As Ricki looked on helplessly she screamed in terror at the atrocious event, not quick enough to intervene. The site of blood was extensive.....

CHAPTER 46

Fading in and out of consciousness Brooke managed to discern tiny glimpses of people surrounding her. Feeling herself lying down she was certainly the centre of attention. She knew despite being largely unaware of things. Together with Ricki there were members of public who encircled her first of all, followed by Paramedics. She felt herself suspended onto a stretcher, her body covered with a blanket, her neck supported. Fading out once again she sensed herself in a room, a room on wheels with a loud siren and a strange mask attached to her face. Though her presence went unnoticed Ricki stuck to her like glue through the whole ordeal, hysterical at the site of her sister's condition. Within no time she was rushed to hospital. Being met immediately by hospital staff and doctors her bed was rolled out the back of the ambulance and in through the main entrance. Patience and visitors were ushered to one side as she was thrust along the corridor to the A&E department. Reaching the operating room doctors scrambled around her. One member of staff aggressively encouraged Ricki to wait outside. Undeterred at first Ricki eventually gave in and stayed back. As the doctors operated she stood for several minutes eager to hear news until eventually deciding to sit on the nearby chair. Heavily sedated by this time Brooke was at this point completely devoid of any consciousness. Her possessions were now safely under the ownership of Ricki who sat on the chair clenching her bag and belongings intensely. After several minutes wait one of the doctors, a young lady of asian origin came out the room where Brooke was being attended and approached Ricki. Having sighted the doctor early Ricki shot up from out of her seat. Advancing towards her Ricki met the doctor halfway with much eagerness.

'What's happening?' she asked her.

'Your sister has suffered severe head injuries. She is currently undergoing an emergency CT scan which will be followed by an MRI' said the doctor. 'We have already seen that she has fractured her skull but we need to ascertain the exact extent of her injuries internally. It's likely she has suffered a cerebral bleed in her brain caused by the head trauma. Her condition is very serious indeed and I feel I must tell you that she may not survive. You should prepare for the worst.'

Ascertaining what the doctor had said Ricki gasped in horror. Sounding more sympathetic as she finished her sentence the doctor continued 'She has a number of other wounds including possible internal bleeding of her organs, a broken leg, broken arm and serious bruising but her head injury is the most serious of all. I'm so sorry.'

Flooded with tears of sorrow before the doctor even finished her sentence Ricki managed to speak as best she could.

'What can I do?' she asked her.

'I'm afraid there is nothing you can do at this time except sit and wait.' replied the doctor. We are doing all we can for her at this time and will keep you up to date with everything.' She added.

Sitting back down as the doctor walked away Ricki put her hands on her face. Sobbing relentlessly she sat alone in the waiting room, no-one there to comfort or consul her. Rightly or wrongly she blamed herself in part for her failure to save her sister which made her suffering worse still. Had she been ever so slightly quicker she would have been able to grab her and stop her from falling down the stairs. Torturing herself with all different ways she could have stopped this from happening she sat lonely and afraid clutching on to her sister's belongings.

Time passed and the minutes turned to hours. Exhausted from her ordeal Ricki eventually fell asleep.

CHAPTER 47

Piercing through the window of a young lady's bedroom the morning sun shone through. The curtains being unable to hold it back the glow from outside slowly lit up the room. Under her duvet Brooke lay asleep, peaceful and cosy in her favourite pyjamas. The morning light slowly penetrated the window and made the darkness disappear. Stirring comfortably in her warm bed Brooke's peaceful slumber turned to a relaxing doze. She lay still without any cares or responsibility, a slight grin appearing on her face.

Sitting up in bed she looked forward to the start of a brand new day. She pulled back the duvet, turned and rose to her feet. Making fists with her toes she felt the velvety soft carpet across her soles and under her heel. The strands of floor covering stroked in between her toes as she gazed down. She walked to the door and left her room, along the hallway and entered the kitchen. There was no sign of Ricki yet. She was most likely still in bed as usual. Peering outside through the kitchen window Brooke poured herself some coffee and switched on the radio. It was bright and sunny outside already, like the start of a hot summer's day.

A somewhat resounding crackling noise was heard from the radio first of all followed by the familiar voice of a friendly DJ. Listening to the radio host introduce the next song she sat down at the table with her cup in hand and began to read the newspaper. Feeling somewhat peckish Brooke grabbed a snack from the cupboard. Tucking in to her breakfast bar she sat back down and continued to read her newspaper. The DJ's voice was overheard as Brooke studied the newspaper.

'Good morning listeners, and for all of you who have just woken up from the glare of sunlight through your window curtains while you were in your nice warm bed I've got just the song for you comin' up. So make sure you're wearing your favourite pyjamas, pour yourself some coffee, relax and have a good old read of the newspaper while you eat a cereal bar out the cupboard. Hope you're having a truly fun start to this nice bright summer's day in January!'

The song on the radio was *'Don't Dream it's Over'* by Crowded House which began to play. One story in particular that caught her eye was that of a man who believed himself to be the real Santa Claus. The article was entitled 'Mad Santa'. She also gazed at countless advertisements for everything from Christmas and January sales and promotions to Halloween outfits, fireworks, summer fashion and dream catchers. After having spent several minutes perusing the newspaper Brooke turned off the radio, stood up, poured herself some more coffee and marched to the living room. Perching down on the sofa she grabbed the remote and switched on the TV.

The program on TV was a morning chat show with a young female TV presenter sat down with an elderly overweight man who appeared to be some sort of expert. They were being watched by a live studio audience with a tagline at the bottom of the screen which read *'So you don't know that you're dreaming!'* The two of them were discussing the ins and outs of the significance of dreaming as a way of escaping from reality and how so often the majority of people are completely ignorant of their dream state while they are asleep.

Brooke suddenly felt very uncomfortable. She was hit by with a heightened sense of dread, confusion, fear and worry, all at once. What was happening to her at this time? She had just woken up in bed without remembering climbing in to bed last night. Why was it the start of a hot summer's day in January? Who made the fresh pot of coffee she was drinking when Ricki was still in bed? How did the DJ narrate everything as she was doing it? Who bought the newspaper she was reading and why was it filled with random nonsense that made no sense? And why were there repeated mentions of dreams – the ad in the paper, the song on the radio and now the TV show.

Continuing to watch the two people chatting away on TV Brooke witnessed something that terrified her in a way that she had never felt before. The female presenter and her guest ceased their discussion and turned to the camera as an awkward silence filled the whole TV studio, as well as the living room. Breaking the fourth wall the presenter stared intently at the screen for a few moments then spoke. 'Brooke you're dreaming my dear' she announced.

A freezing cold chill ran through her spine at the sight of what she just witnessed. Grasping the remote in her hand Brooke immediately reacted the only way she knew how and switched the TV off.

Standing up to her feet she dashed out the living room. She had to get out!! She thought to herself after promptly making her way towards the front door of her flat only to be met by another terrifying site she slammed against the doorway.

Covering the entire width of the exit was a giant steel bolt that was held in place with a large rustic looking padlock. The lock was bolted tightly to the front door and could not be removed. Where the hell had this come from? She certainly didn't remember having it installed. Shaking the door and banging rigorously she tried in vain to push her way free. Her attempt was fruitless. The door was sealed shut and there was no way out.

Giving up after just a few moments she stood still beside the door and thought about her predicament. Was this really a dream? If it was then perhaps that was some comfort. After all she had just witnessed someone talk to her through an electrical appliance in the living room. It was reminiscent of a scene from a recent horror movie. Closing her eyes she slowly began to compose herself. Hands still shaking with terror she took several deep breaths and managed to calm herself down a little. If this really was a dream it was unlike any other she had ever experienced before. Having had no memory of falling asleep or going to bed beforehand left her in a state of confusion.

CHAPTER 48

Lying unconscious in her hospital bed Brooke's appearance was that of a peaceful demeanour. A far cry from what was happening to her internally. Her head in bandages and her leg and arm in plaster she lay still with Ricki sat by her side. Stubbornly refusing to leave her sister Ricki sat whispering in her ear words of comfort and support just hoping for a reaction. Her endeavours so far had proven unsuccessful. Brooke was as unresponsive as she was silent. Looking at her watch Ricki read the time as 1.03 AM. They had been in hospital for over 13 hours but it felt like a lifetime. Unsure as to whether her sister would ever wake up despite having survived so far at least.

Due to her thoughts being occupied by her sister Ricki felt she should catch some more sleep but was incapable at this time. She decided instead to look through the contents of Brooke's bag. Her purse, phone and keys all present she was keeping them safe for her sister in the hope of handing them all back to her soon. She switched Brooke's phone on and perused her menu. Being her usual nosy self she read through her texts messages and recent call history but saw nothing of particular interest. Spying her Notes app she decided to open it and read the most recent entry. The words subway, roundabout, Kingston Hospital and 12.10AM. What was this she had put on her phone? Was this the time and location of the next accident? If so with her sister being completely incapacitated she would have to try and prevent it herself.

Longing to contact their friends and family Ricki decided it was far too late and instead to do so in the morning. On reflection there was one person who she thought would be of particular use to come and visit - a person whose presence here could prove vital in assisting with Brooke's recovery.

CHAPTER 49

Hours passed and night soon turned to morning. Asleep in the armchair next to her sister's bed Ricki woke up as the doctor walked in to check on Brooke. Tired and dazed Ricki rubbed her eyes and glanced over at the doctor for his reaction.

'How is she doing?' Ricki asked. 'We're still unsure at this time' replied the doctor. 'We have run some tests but can't agree on our findings. Her neural brain activity appears to be extremely active for someone who's unconscious. It's like she's still wide awake. As for the internal bleeding, only time will tell' he added.

Ricki had work to do that day. Having decided there was only one person besides her who should visit Brooke she decided to collect her things together and head out. Having said goodbye to Brooke and that she'll be back later she kissed her gently on the forehead and left her sleeping. She headed straight out the hospital and caught a taxi home. Without time to waste she entered the flat, put both their mobile phones on charge and made herself some coffee. This was her fuel needed for the day. Having been in dire need of freshening up she had a prompt shower followed by a speedy change of clothes.

Less than fifteen minutes passed in which she came and left the house though not before booking another taxi. She had one very important location she needed to go before heading back to visit Brooke in hospital.

CHAPTER 50

Seated still on her sofa Brooke was still in a state of disbelief at her predicament and though now relatively calm she thought to herself about how she could possibly be in this unique situation. What had happened beforehand that led to this point? Why was she unable to escape the house? If she was really dreaming then where was she in reality? She realised she most likely wasn't asleep in her own bed, but where? Her memory was extremely hazy. Putting her hands over her face and staring at the floor in concentration she heard a voice from very close by that sounded familiar.

'Hello Brooke' the voice said gently.

Startled she looked up to the armchair on her left to see a face she recognised. She saw a tall gaunt looking man with white hair. It was Dr Barack Gorman.

'Hello Brooke' he said again, this time looking her directly in the face.

'I've been asked by your sister Ricki to come and see you. I'm sitting by your bed in hospital. She's here too. You were in an accident. You fell and hurt yourself.'

Using a technique I've perfected over the years I'm attempting to talk to you through the power of dream walking. That's the ability to enter someone's dream state and talk to them while they're asleep or unconscious. As you know even while you're asleep, many of your senses are still functional and your ears never really turn off. You still hear everything around you even while you dream and what you hear will absolutely influence your subconscious. That's why I know you can hear me now, and if I'm guessing right you can probably see me too, or at least your own mental projection of me.'

Startled at first by what the doctor told her his words slowly became somewhat comforting to Brooke and everything began to make more sense. With so much more to tell Brooke the doctor continued.

'The young lady who can predict the future in her dreams!' he said.

Brooke's reaction to what the doctor said was that of shock and surprise at first. How did he know this? She thought to herself.

'Your sister told me everything' he added. 'And following much doubt and disbelief and a lot of arguing she eventually managed to convince me of what you've been able to do in your dreams. In all my years in this profession I've never heard of anything so extraordinary. Certainly nothing that's not magic or supernatural that's been proven. I am a scientist after all and I believe that everything can be explained rationally. And although your ability had me bamboozled at first I have since come up with something that might possibly resemble a rational explanation. I know this might be a lot for you to take in at this time, particularly when considering your situation right now but your sister and I believe that explaining this to you might assist your recovery.'

Brooke sat back on the sofa as the doctor continued.

'You are an extremely intelligent lady. I discussed your test results from the other day with my colleague who was equally astounded as I. Your IQ is off the chart as were your Theta Wave readings. It was already my belief that high insight causes lucid dreaming and that lucid dreaming causes an increase in insight, or to put it quite simply the more you dream the more intelligent you become and the more intelligent you become the more you dream. I believe that the subconscious section of our brain records everything we hear, see and feel. In most people only a fraction of this is transferred to the conscious part of our minds but in your case I believe that your subconscious is somehow communicating with your conscious mind through the power of your dreams. In your case so far it has prioritized the most important aspects to communicate as the unnecessary loss of human life. I know that you worked as a market analyst processing vast amounts of numerical, social, political and scientific data in your last job. Your superior intellect and education have put you at the top of your class in every subject you ever studied and you have a wealth of knowledge.'

Seated still on the sofa and hearing it all with great intrigue Brooke listened with undivided attention as the doctor continued further.

'Somehow all this knowledge in your mind has been analysed, disseminated, processed and sent to your conscious mind. If this is true then it is a truly staggering achievement. What we're talking about here is the pinpoint accuracy of an almost infinite number of calculations and variables in your mind that enables you to predict the exact future outcome of events. I've noticed that all the places you have predicted these events are places that you've known and are familiar with. Your subconscious has been taking notes everywhere you've been, even at times when you weren't really paying attention your mind has been absorbing everything you've seen and heard like a giant sponge and then piecing it all together like a big four-dimensional puzzle.'

Hearing every word the doctor said Brooke remained in silence pondering further on her situation and whether she was ever going to escape it.

'I'm afraid I must leave you to rest now' said the doctor. 'I fear I may have overloaded you with too much information so I'll leave it there for the time being but your sister has asked me to come back tomorrow which I'm happy to do' he added.

With those words the doctor vanished from Brooke's view leaving her alone in her living room.

CHAPTER 51

Brooke continued to sit in silence pondering to herself about the current situation.

With Brooke's attention turning away for a moment she heard another voice speak aloud. She turned back towards where the doctor had previously been seated only moments before to see an all too familiar site. It was a middle aged woman who bore an uncanny resemblance to her.

'Hello Brooke' she said out aloud.

Turning her attention back towards her the impact at the sight of this woman left Brooke astounded. As she sat as large as life before her she could not believe her eyes.

'Mum!?' she said out allowed.

'Hello my dear' said her mother. 'It's been a long time' she added while smiling tenderly at her.

Brooke then remembered her place. She was dreaming. This wasn't happening.

'You're not real' said Brooke shaking her head.

'Am I not!?' replied her mother with a slightly sarcastic tone.

'No you're just an illusion, a manifestation caused by my subconscious'

'Much like the doctor just now, was he not real?' said her mother.

'With you it's different' insisted Brooke. 'I know you can't be real since you're dead. You're not sitting down in a chair next to my bed in hospital. I know that much. I wish you were real but I know you're not. You're just a figment of my imagination. You're a character in my dream. My mind is playing tricks on me. That's why I'm trapped in this house in the first place!' she said

'I'm afraid you're gravely mistaken' replied her mother. You should realise that your mind is not playing tricks on you at this time. It's keeping you here for a reason' she added.

'And what reason is that?' asked Brooke.

'Your body is trying to repair itself. If and when it is healed sufficiently it will let you out'

'If that's the case then why are you here?' replied Brooke

'I'm here to help you' she replied. 'Much like you've been helping people lately!' she joked.

'What are you here to help me with?' asked Brooke. 'To help me get out of this place?' she added.

'That's part of it.' her mother replied. 'But I've also come to help you help your sister' she said.

'Ricki? Why does she need my help? She's not the one in hospital'?

'Turn on your TV and find out' said her mother.

Looking somewhat puzzled and reluctant Brooke picked up the remote and switched the TV on as her mother instructed. Brooke looked on as the TV clicked and slowly lit up to reveal a fuzzy looking screen. Continuing to view the screen she turned to her mother looking for answers.

'What are we watching?' she asked

'We're seeing your visions on screen like a real film'. she replied.

'How is this possible?' asked Brooke.

'We're in a dream inside your head!' she replied. 'Anything is possible'

They both looked on as the TV screen began to focus. The image was slowly starting to reveal itself. The picture revealed Ricki. They were watching her at home looking at Brooke's mobile phone. They saw a birds eye view of the screen of her phone as Ricki was flicking through. They saw her reading the texts messages, the recent calls, and the Notes page. The words subway, round-about, Kingston Hospital and 12.10AM.

Looking on at her sister on the TV Brooke became

somewhat worried. The TV screen suddenly went blank for a very brief moment then changed to reveal a different scenario. She watched on seeing Ricki making her way along a busy road junction, a roundabout with exits in all directions. The same junction she had seen in her dream the night before. Then it quickly became apparent. This was another premonition. Ricki was going to try and stop the accident that Brooke had foreseen, except this time she was going to do it alone without her sister's guidance. Continuing to watch on Brooke saw Ricki approach the junction, though from the opposite side to where the young lady was crossing. Ricki could be seen catching sight of the lady and attempt to cross the street.

Brooke knew the outcome. She was about to try and save the life of the young lady at the cost of her own. She had changed the outcome of her future by seeing the notes on Brooke's phone. Brooke could watch no longer. Grasping at the remote she promptly pointed the device at the TV and switched it off.

In anger and frustration she turned to her mother. 'Why did you make me watch that!?' she demanded.

'This is why I came to see you' her mother replied. 'Your sister now needs your help just as you've needed hers.'

'Is this for certain?' asked Brooke. 'Is this definitely going to happen?' she added.

'You know that you've never been wrong about your predictions' replied her mother.

'Then why I didn't I see this happen in the first place?' she insisted.

'You've changed the outcome by being here in this place. I don't think you predicted this part of it would happen'. 'You are still a beginner after all' said her mother. 'They say that psychics ironically can never predict their own misfortunes' she added.

'And how do I know that you're even real?' declared Brooke.

'You don't' replied her mother. 'I'm just a vision in your dreams remember!? But you should know better than anyone that dreams and reality can often be the same thing. You're gifted as we know you always have been, but it's only now that you're starting to see your true potential, and you've barely scratched the surface of what you're truly capable of.'

'Tell me something that proves to me you're real then' demanded Brooke.

'I remember one day when you were a very small child. You couldn't even walk or talk at the time but I saw you show the first true sign of who you really are. We sat on the floor to do one of your jigsaw puzzles together. I got up to answer the door.

When I came back you had completed the puzzle all by yourself. Later that day we were at the park. You saw a woman crying on the park bench and crawled over to her with your arms out to cuddle and comfort her. You showed me the two most important sides to your character in one day.' said her mother smiling.

'That doesn't prove to me that you're real.' insisted Brooke. 'Tell me something I don't know that proves you're more than just a part of my dream' she added.

Looking back at Brooke, her mother laughed and began to explain.

'Under the floor boards below my wardrobe' she explained.

'What!?' Exclaimed Brooke with a mixture of shock and surprise.

'It was the only way Ricki could outsmart you when you were kids was by getting help from me and your father. One day when you went out he cut the floor boards out below our wardrobe to remove and made a small hole, just big enough for her to hide in. You never found her again after. We helped her outsmart you without you ever knowing and told her never to reveal the secret, or even mention our involvement.' she said.

'I still don't believe it' declared Brooke.

'At this time it's of minor importance and

you shouldn't concern yourself too much with whether I'm real or not. Time is running out, you need to get out of her and help the person you care about the most. That issue is very real' replied her mother.

CHAPTER 52

Continuing her conversation with her mother sitting opposite Brooke continued to enquire.

'What will happen if I don't get out of this place on time?' she asked.

'Switch on your TV again and find out' replied her mother

Brooke picked up the remote again, pointing the device at the TV she pressed the ON button and the TV powered up. She saw another familiar sight appear on screen. It was herself, dressed in black wearing a head vail. Was she at a funeral or something? As she watched on her mother began to talk her through it.

'If you don't get out of this place your sister will die, and so will the young lady. Both losses will devastate you for a long time to come. You'll blame yourself, particularly for the person you care most about, and you'll see her loss as a defeat for the first time in your life.' She said

The movie on TV played out as her mother continued to explain. It was indeed Brooke at a funeral, that of Ricki's. Partially obscured by her veil she was teary eyed, surrounded by familiar faces in an altar. The same one as her parents' funeral.

The movie then jumped forward to an alternate time and place, now looking at Brooke's future. She saw herself at work in a stylish office, surrounded by colleagues. Ending in thunderous applause she was giving a speech, beaming with happiness in front of everyone.

The movie then cut to a different setting. A lavish house in the country with two sports cars parked on the grounds outside, her vision now turned to first person Brooke knew this was to be her house in the future. Taking her coat off as she entered the house gave the view of a grand reception area towered over by a large staircase. Underneath the staircase was a hidden door that led to her base of operations. A secret room filled with TV screens, computers and desks. A large round table could be seen on one side.

Then to another setting, Brooke bumped into a man on the train on her way to work. Later that day she bumped into him again. Laughing together they had a date.

Then forward to another setting, a wedding, her wedding with the same man, then her in the hospital, the man by her side with a baby crying.

More images appeared, her playing with her child,

reading to him, chasing him around the garden, and the child's birthday party.

The movie then cut to a photo of Ricki on the mantelpiece. Staring at it sentimentally Brooke could be seen picking the photo up to study the image in depth. A tear could be seen in her eye as she lowered the photo back down.

Her mother carried on with her commentary on the movie as it all played out.

'You will survive and endure. You will become successful in so many ways and you will change the world for the better. You will even find true happiness, but you will miss her always and will never stop blaming yourself' she said.

As the movie ended the screen went blank. Brooke pointed the remote at the screen once again and switched the TV off.

Brooke sat in silence for a moment, eyes still gazed on the blank screen. Turning to her mother she began to talk.

'I've already lost you and dad, I'm not going to lose her too!' she insisted. 'Now tell me how the hell do I get out of her!?' she demanded.

'That's one question you no longer need my help with!' replied her mother

A sudden realization came over Brooke. She understood once again that she was the one who was in control, just as she always has been. She leapt to her feet and walked to the door of the living room turning around to speak to her mum one last time.

'I miss you so much!' she said to her emotionally.

'Give my love to your sister too' replied her mother.

With that Brooke raced out the room, along the hallway and down the stairs towards the front door. Her fist clenched tight she approached the door with all emotions running high and a look of shear rage and determination on her face. She pulled her fist back then struck the door with all her strength. The force with which she thumped the door was well beyond what any human being was capable of in the real world. She struck the door in the centre of the large steel girder that covered it. The resulting smash hit the spot with such speed and ferocity that the entire doorway was prised clean off all its hinges and propelled backwards, girder still attached. As the doorway flew open a dazzling white light shone in on Brooke blinding her from any other vision.

CHAPTER 53

All alone in her hospital bed her head still draped in bandages and two of her limbs in plaster Brooke lay quiet and peaceful in her sleep. All of a sudden she began to twitch. She almost immediately opened her eyes with a gasp and leaned forward. She had successfully escaped from her dream and was now back to reality.

Gazing down at her body to see the plaster mould on her arm she was in a certain state of shock. Pulling her blanket sheets off her she looked down at the rest of her body and saw her broken leg on top of a small frame. This too was covered in plaster. She was virtually immobolised. What was she going to do now? She couldn't walk anywhere and she certainly couldn't run. Now mindful of all the tubes inserted in her body all over she would also need to remove these first before she moved anywhere.

She looked all around her intensive care room and even through the small window into the ward. She saw no one around at this time. No doctors or nurses who could assist. Probably for the better as there was no way they would let her out in her condition and she decided she was better off alone for now.

Brooke remembered her predicament. She had no time to waste. The clock was ticking, and even if she arrived at the accident on time would she have to choose who to save? With two of her limbs incapacitated it meant she effectively had just one arm and leg to use. Brooke was not going to let that stop her. She decided she was going to have to get to where her sister was even if she had to hop all the way there on one foot. Feeling the bandages on her head she decided to leave them alone as they wouldn't affect her mobility after all. She pulled the blankets off her body completely, threw them to the floor then gently removed the frame under her broken leg which fell to the floor on the opposite side. Sitting up straight she twisted her body and legs to the side and was now seated on the edge of the bed. She gently lowered her good leg to the floor. With her foot flat on the tiles she slowly shifted her weight on to her leg and stood up cautiously.

She had to get out of there. Her attention fixed on the door she began to hop with one foot while using the wall to help balance. Brooke approached the door of her room and while looking through the small window at the top slowly began to turn the handle. Balanced on one foot she pulled the door inwards and pushed it open completely. Peering her head around the doorway she glanced left, then right. There was still no sign of anyone. She could only make out the distant voices of several doctors in conversation with a patient in another room and a nurse in the bathroom with someone else.

Hopping out of the room she made her way down the corridor to the reception desk. Luckily for her it was un-manned. Already feeling exhausted from trotting one-footed all this distance she looked around the desk for anything that might assist. She saw the usual equipment around the desk such as bandages, medicine bottles and papers but nothing of any use. She then turned her attention back to the hallway and noticed something of great interest. A few metres along resting against the wall stood a set of underarm crutches. Did these belong to the other patient in the bathroom? In any case this was exactly what she needed. Hopping over to the crutches she grabbed one and placed it under her good arm. Fortunately her broken leg and arm were on opposite sides. Had both damaged limbs been on one side of her body the crutch would have been of little or no use to her. She tested the crutch out by making one step with her weight on it then resting herself on her good leg. Repeating the process again she was happy with how it was working. It was far from ideal but was much more practical than hopping everywhere. Brooke had now gained a significant advantage in her mobility. With the crutch comfortably under her arm she quickly made her way further along the corridor towards the ward exit.

Having reached the way out she hit the button on the wall to unlock the door. Pushing it wide open she was able to crutch-walk through the exit before the door sprung back.

Continuing along the corridor and noting that she was on the second floor of the hospital she made her way to the lift. Arriving at the lift doors she pushed the button which lit up then waited anxiously. The lift could be heard rising to her floor from below then after a few seconds the doors opened and she made her way in. She pushed the button for the ground floor and the lift went down. Upon arriving at the floor below the doors opened again to reveal another corridor leading to the hospital exit.

Brooke exited the lift and continued along the ground floor corridor. She caught sight of several doctors in conversation with each other and a queue of people at the reception desk, none of whom paid any real attention to her.

She raced out the hospital entrance, along the street towards the big roundabout. As she made her way to her intended location she came across a familiar sight. Walking towards her was someone she recognised. A tall, gaunt looking man with grey hair, it was doctor Gorman. On his way to visit her for a second time no doubt. Having caught sight of her he quickly increased his pace towards her with a look of shock and desperation. As he approached Brooke he began to talk while Brooke continued to move in her direction.

'What are you doing!? You're supposed to be recovering in hospital!' he told her with much apprehension.

'I need your help!' insisted Brooke. 'I now have two lives to save!' she added.

Having realised that Brooke wasn't stopping he turned to walk and talk alongside her. Relentless in her pace Brooke explained her predicament to the doctor as they raced along the street. Trying to offer her assistance with walking at first he soon realised she was better left on her own with that.

'I know all about your little gift of foresight' He told her. 'I came here yesterday and explained it to you and your sister while you were unconscious' he added.

'I know' Replied Brooke. 'I heard you' she added.

'You heard everything I said to you yesterday!?' he asked

'I did' she replied.

CHAPTER 54

They soon approached the roundabout from the east side. This was unfortunate as the two accidents were about to happen on the north and south side. The only way the north side could be accessed safely by pedestrians was through the tunnel that ran directly from the south end.

Only stopping very briefly to talk and point her finger at the various locations Brooke began to give the doctor clear instructions.

'You can move much faster than I can. We're running out of time. You have to run ahead through the subway to the opposite end and out on the north side. When you see the girl you have to stop her. You must not let that girl cross the road no matter what!' she told him.

'What are you going to do!?' he asked Brooke

'I'm going to save my sister!' she insisted.

Acknowledging Brooke's instructions the doctor ran on ahead leaving her on her own to stumble towards the location of Ricki's accident. Despite her exhaustion and anxiety at this moment being at the highest she had ever felt and her sister's life now in her hands she continued undeterred.

She approached the south side of the roundabout to see a familiar face approach from the other direction. A young lady about 5'6" with long blond hair wearing trousers and a hoody, it was Ricki. She hadn't noticed Brooke at this time. Her attention focused on the passing cars she was watching.

Brooke's exhaustion made her attempts to call out to her sister futile. Several endeavours to shout her name proved completely fruitless. Having no other choice but to restrain her physically Brooke persisted instead with racing towards her.

Ricki approached the kerb line looking directly across the roundabout at the location of the young lady, still completely unaware of Brooke approaching. With the intention to cross very much on her mind she was about to step out on to the road when all of a sudden she felt an arm grab her from behind. She felt herself fall back as the arm tightened its grip around her. Before even having a moment to react she felt herself falling to the ground on top of another person. While falling she noticed a leg in plaster on one side and a crutch swing towards her front. What the hell was going on!? She thought to herself.

Ricki turned around astonished to see Brooke's face, her head still covered in bandages. Brooke still lacking the energy to speak properly and gasping for breath simply pointed to the opposite side of the roundabout. Ricki acknowledged her sister's motions and gazed across the street for herself.

Looking on as Doctor Gorman could be seen across the road approaching the young lady the sisters both watched in anticipation. An argument seemed to ensue after the doctor appeared to speak to the young lady, all in silence to the two sisters due to the distance and clamour of traffic. He could then be seen blocking her access to crossing the street and continued to barricade her off from the kerbside. Eventually giving in after a minute or so she walked towards the subway. She turned around once when she was at a distance from the doctor and appeared to shout obscenities. The doctor appeared to have been successful.

Still laying on top of her sister Ricki's attention veered back to Brooke. She turned back to face her.

'What the hell are you doing here!?' she asked her.

'Saving your dumb arse!' replied Brooke falling to her back feeling crippled with exhaustion.

EPILOGUE

The next day Ricki and Doctor Gorman went back to visit Brooke who was lying safely in her hospital bed in intensive care. Her leg and arm were given a new plaster cast and her head bandages were replaced with new ones. Brooke was explaining the events of the last 24 hours to both Ricki and Doctor Gorman who were seated on opposite sides of her bed.

'I got a very bad telling off by the doctors for leaving yesterday' declared Brooke. They said this morning that they were astounded at my level of progress though. They said at this rate I could make a full recovery within a month'. she added.

'That's great news!' said Ricki. 'So did you have any more nightmares last night?' she added.

'No I think my mind's taking a rest from all of that for the time being, but I'm sure it'll come back soon though' said Brooke.

'When it does come back we'll ready for it' Insisted Ricki.

Brooke nodded in agreement.

'I thought I should also let you know that I opened your letter you received from about the interview last week and they've offered you the job' declared Ricki.

'That's nice to know!' replied Brooke. 'It's almost a shame that I don't need it now' she added.

Laughing at her sister's comment Ricki then looked on insistently at Brooke. 'Now about your dream, tell me more about what mum said to you!' she said.

'I told you it was just a dream Ricki! She told me some nonsense about how you used to hide under the floor boards below the wardrobe when we were kids' said Brooke.

Upon hearing what her sister said Ricki's reaction was to look at her mortified as if she had just seen a ghost.